You Should Get That Looked At

S. Craig Renfroe, Jr.

Main Street Rag Publishing Company
Charlotte, NC

Cover art: *Synopsis of Asylum* by Christine Cassano
Book design and layout by M. Scott Douglass
Author photo on back cover by Chris Renfroe

Acknowledgments:

The following stories first appeared in slightly different forms in the accompanying publications:
"Janine's Dead": *The MacGuffin*
"Mistletoe Hunt" and "In the Dark": *Seedhouse*
"Off the Pier": *Atlantis*
"Tickle, Me?": *One Paycheck Away* (Main Street Rag, 2003)

With special thanks to Julie Funderburk, Charles Israel, Wendy Waite, Melody Clayton, Alex Clayton, Wendy Brenner, Rebecca Lee, P. Nolan Belk, and Derek Nikitas.

ISBN 1-930907-42-7

Main Street Rag
4416 Shea Lane
Charlotte, NC 28227
www.MainStreetRag.com

Contents

In memory of:

William Burns Renfroe
&
James Mack Tucker

ROMANTIC CUPIDITY

They called it the White House, but that was just because it was white. It'd been a funeral home before the sorority bought it. Rumor said during initiations the sisters locked the pledges up in the embalming room. Edgar got invited to their parties and always dragged me along. We always walked the whole way there.

"You know what the best thing about these parties is?" Edgar asked.

"Free beer?"

"The fact that for a brief time we can all be honest. At these little functions, we all know what we want, and we know what everyone else wants."

"You should change your major to philosophy."

"Clarity." Edgar spun around. "Nothing but naked desire."

Edgar got his desire in the form of a bleached blonde with neon green nails and a shirt that read, "I'm not easily pleased." He tipped an imaginary hat in my direction, and they disappeared into the pulsating heat and crackling white noise of the crowd.

I made my way to the desperate and lonely section of the House, a room full of couches: red ones, green ones, leather ones, coffee-stained ones, cigarette-burnt ones, ones without cushions. A veritable couch graveyard. All the non-dancing, temporarily non-screwing types found their way here. I sat on the couch that looked least urine-stained and focused on my plastic cup of Bud, enjoying the way the little bubbles hugged the edge, afraid to venture out into the middle.

Someone flipped over the back of my couch, elbowing the cup out of my hand and sending my precious Bud to the floor, where it could only hope to stain the carpet in some recognizable image, like Abe Lincoln, so it could achieve some sort of legacy. Bored and belligerent, I grabbed the flipper by the shoulders. A catlike face poked out of dark brown hair at me, but she drew breath like a fish. I helped her upright.

"Love me," she said.

A strange thank you, I thought.

"Love me."

She sounded rather demanding that time. "I don't really know you," I said.

"Love me."

"Right here?"

"Love me."

"I'm not good at these awkward moments."

"Love me."

"You aren't listening, are you?"

"Love me."

"When I'm down and blue, all I want is someone to..."

"Love me."

I thought she might be stuck. I figured it had to be some drug-induced state of romantic cupidity.

"You know I took LSD once," I said. "It made me feel this scratching in my leg and when I looked down, there was a hole in my thigh, this place where a crawfish had dug into my leg." I shuddered; I could still feel that crawfish. "I never took acid again."

"Love me," she said, sounding sympathetic.

The next day, Ms. Malpass wore black hose to our poetry seminar and as always a skirt and jacket, all uniformly dark. We thought she was Croatian or of some Baltic descent, though you could only hear the strains of an accent come through when, excited or angry, she over-stressed a word. According to reliable rumor, her family was killed in some terrible act of ethnic cleansing. No one knew how she got to America, much less the little private college Lossdor, but with all her relatives gone, she lived close to campus in a huge colonial house, alone. In class, Ms. Malpass acted as if we were the enemy and she were being forced to reveal her secrets. Sometimes in mid-sentence she'd stop, look at one of us, and back away with an expression of utter distaste. It was hard not to take it personally.

"What you have to realize." Pause. "What you have to realize is that every poem. Every poem." She paced back and forth. "*Every* poem is a plot against the reader."

She walked to the blackboard and wrote the words in huge letters in her neat spiraling script. Her body almost shaped the letters as she wrote them. She turned to face us. That look. She targeted it at Alex Limpkin in the front row, his pudgy and attentive face drawing up in the spotlight of her gaze.

"Mr. Limpkin, what do you think T. S. Eliot is trying to do in 'The Wasteland.'"

"I think he was trying to show us the breakdown of modern society," Limpkin said.

Edgar snorted. We hated Limpkin's visceral aptitude, his eagerness to read all the assignments, talk to the professors, kiss all the asses.

"Of course you'd think that; you're a man," she said.

Some of the girls shuffled their feet and improved their posture, perhaps afraid she would call on one of them.

"And a weak reader," she continued in on Limpkin. "You don't see Eliot's manipulation, his contrivance to force the reader to see women as hysterical, broken. When in truth he was the hysterical one, the one who suffered emotional breakdowns. Don't you see the writer's ability to twist your will, bend your emotions to his purpose?"

"Yes, Ms. Malpass." Limpkin's face was burning.

Edgar laughed.

Ms. Malpass swivelled her head toward our side of the room. "Mr. Kenningston, stay after class."

"Edgar, you mean, ma'am?" I asked.

"No."

"But, ma'am, he was the one who laughed."

"And you're the one I'm asking to stay after."

"Yes ma'am."

"You write, don't you, Mr. Kenningston?"

"No ma'am."

"Ms. Malpass, please."

"No, Ms. Malpass. I just read."

"Aren't you involved with that Quad Poetry Reading."

"Yes, but I read other people's poems."

"Really?" She put her red nailed finger to her pale lips and stared at me.

I blinked a few times, wondering what it was I should

do. Finally, she turned from me and walked over to the board and started erasing it. I guessed I was dismissed.

Edgar was right outside the door. "What'd she want?"

"She wanted to know if I wrote poetry."

"You're plotting against her."

"Funny."

"Every poem is a plot against the reader, you know."

"I told her I only read poetry."

"What else?" He did a pirouette to impress one of the White House sisters looking his way.

"That's it. She got this far away look, and I apparently disappeared."

"You're no threat. I think I'll start writing."

"Better start with nursery rhymes."

"If you wish to live and thrive, let the spider walk alive."

The next Quad reading was that night, and I planned on reading a William Blake poem like an evangelical preacher conjuring the fires of Hell. Edgar promised to come, but as good as his word, he had yet to show. We read under the statue of Duran Ruddy, one of the university's esteemed benefactors, and the guy up before me finished his new poem and with typical collegiate pretense was burning it at Ruddy's bronze feet. We had a nice crowd, around twenty, not counting the readers. Some of them even clapped as the pyro poet descended.

The brick dais the statue stood on required extra navigation because it sloped up narrowly, and I'd worn my loafers, no traction, but they went with the outfit.

Once I'd gained the high ground, I flipped to the poem in my leather-bound poetry anthology and peeked out at my sullen audience, only to spy the Love-me Girl, sitting on the outskirts under a water oak, staring at me as if I were about to self-immolate. No reason to care, I told myself.

I stood straight, took in the air, rank as it was with Ruddy's chicken processing plant down the road, and said, "I'd like to read a quickie by William Blake called 'I Asked a Thief':

"I asked a thief to steal me a peach,
He turned up his eyes;
I ask'd a lithe lady to lie her down,
Holy & meek she cries."

The Love-me Girl's look changed to someone finding a snake in the garage. She shut the text-book in her lap, stood, and walked over to the back of the crowd. In her walk, I felt a kind of contract between the two of us, but I wasn't sure I wanted to sign.

"As soon as I went
An angel came.
He wink'd at the thief
And smild at the dame–"

The Girl smiled. But what did that smile mean: that preacher's voice of mine sure is funny, she really likes this turn in the poem, she wants me, my fly is open, her face muscles are tired of frowning?

"And without one word said
Had a peach from the tree
And still as a maid
Enjoy'd the lady."

Perfunctory applause; the pyro flicked his Bic as if he

were at a heavy metal concert. I caught something out of the corner of my eye, a quick movement, almost a run. A woman with long dark hair, dressed all in black, ducking into Burton Hall, the language building, away from the center of the Quad but within hearing. Ms. Malpass?

Back on the ground, I wanted to talk to the Love-me Girl, but I couldn't think of a thing to ask her. Then she accosted me.

"I liked the poem. Did you write it?"

"No, it's by William Blake." She wasn't a good listener.

"Oh. I really liked the way you read it."

"Thanks." I bowed my head to look humble and sheepish. She had her textbook in her hand, her place marked by an index finger. *The Norton Anthology of Romantic and Victorian Literature*. Odd, she didn't seem the English type. I leaned in closer to her–most men do that to peek down a woman's shirt, and there I was trying to get a peek at a page number. Two twenty-three. Remember two twenty-three.

"My name is Irene."

"Oh, I'm Brett. Kenningston."

"Nice to meet you," she said.

"Well, we met that night."

"What night?"

"When you kept saying 'love me.'"

"I don't remember that."

"I should say not." I had the horrid lucidity to realize what I was saying. "Or maybe it was someone else."

She only nodded.

"So I looked it up, and do you know what was on two twenty-three?"

Edgar yawned elaborately. "No. But it better have something to do with sex."

"It was some of William Blake's poetry, and do you know what poem was on that specific page?"

"Quit with the leading questions already."

"The poem I read. The same one."

"So."

"How did she know?"

"Did you tell anyone?"

"No."

"You told me."

"Did you tell her?"

"No." Edgar got up and opened the mini-fridge; empty as always. "What does it matter?"

"Ok, but why would she lie to me? She knew perfectly well who that poem was by."

"Maybe she was flirting with you. Ever think of that?"

"Fine. Make light of the situation." He was right, the bastard. Still, I wanted it to be more.

The thing I liked most about Lossdor U. was the way the giant oaks made shadow pools on the newly cut grass, deep dark oases amid desert green. I walked through one of those pools thinking how I'd like to bring Irene here and hide.

"What is a reader?" Ms. Malpass asked.

Limpkin said, "Someone who can see that all poems are plots against them."

She didn't even acknowledge he'd spoken. "What does it take to read against the author?" She scanned the classroom, students' eyes dashing down as her gaze swept by. "Mr. Kenningston?"

Dammit. "What's a reader?" I said. That's right, I thought, stall.

Ms. Malpass tapped her index finger on her podium, waiting.

"A reader. I suppose a reader is as much an interpreter as someone who soaks up what the writer writes."

"So you don't subscribe to the tabula rasa theory? We're not just blank slates on which writers imprint their thoughts?" she asked.

"No. Like when I read at the Quad. I can read the same poem seriously or funny. It depends on the slant I want to give it."

Ms. Malpass stopped her tapping and looked at me, not with that expression of disgust or her continuous gaze of sullen indifference but something else, like she was looking at me under a microscope and I'd started to replicate. The stare went on longer than her usual fare, and the class took notice, paper was shuffled, pens dropped, coughs coughed, chairs creaked. I began to sweat.

Without taking her eyes off me, she said, "Class, write seven interpretations of Pound's first Canto for next time. Dismissed." She turned her back on us. Motionless, she stared at the blank blackboard.

"Limpkin's dead," Edgar said.

"What?"

"Killed himself."

"How?"

"Jumped. Four stories. He died on the way to the hospital."

"Why would he do that?" I wanted to walk through the shadow on the wall.

"A girl."

"Girl?"

"His girlfriend dumped him."

"What a stupid thing to kill yourself over."

"I don't know. He sure showed her."

Friday, my first two classes were canceled in memory of Limpkin. But though she wore more black than usual, Ms. Malpass didn't mention him, omitting his name in the roll call. A third of the class didn't show, and Ms. Malpass didn't ask us any questions, lecturing as if alone. But she did glance at me, dart me quick looks; at least, to my paranoid reading of the situation, she spent an inordinate amount of time staring off into space and at me.

Once the leak began, paranoia flooded over me. Thoughts about Irene not remembering me, or pretending not to remember me, and her extraordinary lack of knowledge about the poem I'd read. And thoughts about Limpkin. Like: did Limpkin jump or was he pushed? A bit too paranoid, probably brought on by my feelings of guilt–the kind of guilt where you're trashing a washed-up celebrity, and someone turns to you and says it's not cool to make fun of dead people. Though I knew Limpkin personally, I couldn't connect with his death; it was like he'd dropped out of college–for instance, I could still make terrible puns.

Instead of ending class, Ms. Malpass stood at the end of my row, stared at me, or my general vicinity, and then walked out.

We were eating lunch at Lossdor U's Bull-pit–cleverly named after the school's team, the Bulls–when Edgar leaned over and said, "I've got gonorrhea." We were well away from the crowds, and only ate there so we could watch the ecstatic munching of the female freshman.

"Can I catch it from the shower?" I asked.

"Screw you."

"Not with gonorrhea you don't."

He gave me the finger.

"So who did it?"

"Beats me."

"You going to tell."

"No, I think I'll get the antibiotics and lay low for a while."

"That's been your problem all along, laying low."

I found Irene in the library, deep in the stacks at a tiny table with only one other seat across from her. I sat down as if I didn't notice her.

"Oh, Irene. Hey."

She looked up from her book. "Brett, right?"

"Yeah." Right? What kind of lasting impression was that? "What you reading?"

"Percy Shelley."

"The awful shadow of some unseen Power/ Floats though unseen among us,–visiting/ This various world with as inconstant wing/ As summer winds that creep from flower to flower."

"That's very beautiful."

Say: no, you're beautiful, I thought. "Yes, you're beautiful." Was that close enough?

She hung her head down, out of humility, pity, or disgust I couldn't tell. Then, I realized she'd begun reading again, so I took out my poetry anthology and pretended to look for another poem to give at the next reading.

"Are you busy tomorrow night?" she asked.

"I don't think so."

"There's a party at the White House."

"I can make it. Do you want me to pick you up?"

"Why don't we meet."

Meet, of course, what an idiot, I thought. "Where?"

"How about in the embalming room. Around eight."

"Ok, I've never seen it."

"Doesn't get much traffic."

She kept talking about the mundane minutia that cluttered our college lives, but all I could hear was "love me, love me."

With Edgar in bed, I set out alone, a little early. I wanted to kiss everyone I passed: Sonny, the football jock who claimed to've been raped by a fat girl; Moss, who came back to school after following the Grateful Dead for fifteen years; Kate, Miss Sweet Southern Dumplin '96; and the rest, who I couldn't pick out in a line-up. I loved them all.

The white-washed cinder-block structure seemed terribly inviting to me that night, homey. I wandered around a bit, drank a beer, then had to ask for directions to the room.

The door was pushed to and had a combination lock on it, so I had to get one of the sisters to let me in. Inside, I pulled the door closed, wanting to be alone with my anticipation.

But when I turned around, there was something, someone, covered by a white sheet on the embalming table. Limpkin?

I crept over to the table and gingerly tugged on the sheet. The cover moved to expose hair, bright red hair, long and a little frizzy. A dead drunk sorority sister? I lost my mind before my nerve and yanked the sheet completely off. And there lay a nude window-display mannequin, not anatomically correct but at least curved in all the right places.

Not even getting over that little shock, I heard the door open.

Ms. Malpass stood in the dark of the door. She pushed it closed and started toward me. Where'd she come from, I wondered. What about Irene? Had this been a setup? Irene and Ms. Malpass in on it the whole time, both leading me on. Why, though? But for whatever reason, Irene got me to come here and then let Ms. Malpass close in for the kill. I was losing sight of my insignificance.

"I really enjoy your essays, Mr. Kenningston."

"Thanks."

"But they seem a bit too . . . rigid."

"Really?"

"Almost like you can only think in black and white." She was up against me by then, her whole body touching mine. "You're going to have to learn to recognize the gray."

She put two of her red-tipped fingers to my lips, pressed them there, as if she were trying to quiet me.

"What does a reader do? What does anyone *do*? How can you work against the story of your life?"

I would have said I didn't know, but her fingers were in the way.

"I have to leave," she said. I could've roasted marshmallows off her look.

Think nice thoughts.

Ms. Malpass removed her fingers and in one fluid motion replaced them with her lips. In surprise, I opened my mouth, and in further surprise, I fell back onto the embalming table, and Ms. Malpass followed me down, lips amazingly still attached to mine, more Hoover than woman. She began squirming, writhing. I pushed her dark hair out of my eyes, and there, at the door, was Irene. She stood staring at me, and I was on top of the red-headed mannequin and Ms. Malpass was on top of me, a strange sandwich. I tried to get out from under Ms. Malpass but that just increased her gyration, and I could see from the look in Irene's eyes that it didn't much matter. The mannequin's hard plastic breasts dug into my back so that every time I managed to evade Ms. Malpass's lips, I let out an odd grunt, and before I could find the words to reassure Irene nothing was going on, Ms. Malpass had found my mouth again. Irene stood watching like some repulsively entranced voyeur. Then, she slammed the door.

The noise broke Ms. Malpass's erotic fit. She leapt off me with *that look*–worse than I'd ever seen. I rolled off the embalming table, picked up the mannequin, and held it between us.

"I'm sorry," I said. I felt enormously guilty for some reason.

Without a word she rushed out of the room, a storm of dark colors and pale skin, secrets and shadows.

When I got to the apartment, Edgar was watching Chaplin's *Modern Times* in the dark and drinking vodka straight out of the bottle with ice packs piled around his crotch. The room was bathed in the erratic black-and-white light of the silent movie. I fell into the chair beside the TV.

"So?" he asked.

"Another night at the couch."

"You didn't meet up with her?"

"She never showed."

"Nothing happened?"

"No."

"Well, I still love you."

"Why go on?" I asked in a squeaky voice.

"We'll get by somehow."

Edgar appeared to change with the movements of the TV screen, his face shifting absurdly, a criminal mug shot, a dark lover, a dying youth. I want out, I wanted to say. I want to leave and not come back. Instead, I went to bed.

Monday morning on the way to poetry seminar, we passed clumps of fellow students. Edgar stopped one of the frat boys: "Where you off to, man?"

"No class." The frat boy drifted down the stairs with his friends.

Edgar slapped me on the back. "Hot damn, I can get back to my ice packs."

Edgar left me to stand in the stairwell, wondering what Ms. Malpass was up to. I went to the classroom. The note taped to the wall beside the door said she was ill and had canceled classes for the day. I braved the empty room.

On the blackboard, I wrote, "Every plot is a poem."

S. Craig Renfroe, Jr.

OFF THE PIER

"The longest pier in North Carolina," that's what the sign said. Juniper carried a yellow ten-gallon bucket and the two rods, clicking together in time with the rhythm of her sun-bleached green flip-flops. Keith carried the dung-brown Old Pal tackle box; he said he had to have his hand free to pay for the fishing tickets. Inside, Juniper glanced at the arcade full of teens too young for the bars and clubs but too old for spending time with their parents. A girl around fourteen looked nineteen in a tight black shirt with "Zero" across the chest, an African choker, black lipstick, and green eye-shadow. The girl made a show of staring Keith up and down, from his well-defined calves to his wild ringlets of hair, and then she flashed him a smile. Oblivious, he paid the leathery-skinned attendant behind the counter. The Zero girl gave Juniper a wink as Keith walked toward the pier entrance.

He held the door for Juniper as she piloted the fishing rods out onto the weathered wooden start of the pier, but he walked on by the bucket she held out toward him.

As they walked, she looked at her sun-reddened feet. The planks of the pier passed under them: old dark brownish-gray boards, splintering boards, knotty boards, new weather-proofed green boards.

Keith stopped halfway out onto the pier; farther down, shirtless boys stood shoulder to shoulder with beer-bellied men, stocky black women, and bored-looking preschoolers. He took a rod from Juniper, shook his head at the single hook, and opened the tackle box, looking for a rig.

"What kind of bait did you get?" he asked, still bent over the rod.

"I didn't get any." Juniper looked in the bucket expecting to be surprised by little crabs, flipping shrimp, and darting minnows. A clear, impoverished water stared back up at her. She remembered him going out early that morning with the throw net. "I thought you were going to catch us some."

"Hmm. Well, go get some shrimp. They sell it where we came in at."

She waited for an offer of money, but he was busily studying the other rod, opening and closing the Zebco reel.

The boards creaked, her feet flip-flopped, the birds screeched, and then she was in the shop at the base of the pier. As she approached the leathery man at the counter, the girl in the Zero shirt materialized. With her hair, dyed-black and braided in shoulder length streamers, she looked like some vibrant animal, like a wolverine. Juniper remembered her own painful attempts at adulthood from adolescence: the overzealous makeup, the Winn Dixie parking lot make-out, the terribly short "serious" haircut. Her past still stinging, she almost ran into the Zero girl, who had taken up position between Juniper and the counter.

"Sorry," Juniper said, trying to sidestep the girl.

"You got a smoke?" the girl asked. "Miss?"

"No, I don't smoke."

The girl smiled as if this were something she had over the older woman. Thinking the conversation over, Juniper flip-flopped forward.

"Would you mind if I asked your brother out?" A chorus of laughter followed the question from three girls with kaleidoscope hair and Goodwill clothes, standing near the arcade.

Juniper's thoughts leapt to Aaron somewhere up north in Pennsylvania studying for the bar exam. She focused on an image of him crouched over an enormous book, his circular glasses gradually sliding down his thin nose. Before she could form the question of how the girl knew her brother, Juniper cursed herself. How could she be so stupid?

"He's not my brother."

"Oh, sorry. Boyfriend?"

Juniper didn't answer.

"What's your boyfriend's name?" The girl's hair moved seemingly of its own accord. The three girls by the arcade were almost to their knees in laughter.

"That's none of your business." The Zero girl turned her back on Juniper, elaborately traipsing back, bird-like, to her breathless friends. Juniper stared, expecting the girl to pop little bits of worm into their excited mouths as the group formed a teetering circle. Juniper turned back to the counter and the bait. She told the leathery old man what she wanted, and he begrudgingly got up and moved toward the old refrigerator.

She'd always evaluated older men as grandfathers. She'd never known either of her parent's fathers. The oldest–Grandpa Albert–died from a fall in the Appalachian mountains two weeks after she was born. But this short, sun-baked old man was no grandfather; he was a gruff ex-marine, or sailor, who probably drank till he passed out, caring for nothing except a good dip of snuff and something to complain about.

Across the counter was a full-length mirror that gave the illusion of space. In it, Juniper could see the Zero girl and her satanic acolytes appraising her the way old women eye meat in the supermarket. Juniper followed their gaze. In the mirror image, she saw her auburn hair ravaged by the seawater and tangled in windblown clumps, and her skin oily and red in splotches from the sun. Her figure indefinable in a black t-shirt and green knee-length shorts.

"Two-fifty, lady," the old man said in a tone that sounded as if he'd said it before, but she hadn't been paying attention.

Shrimp in hand, Juniper ignored the Zero girl's crowd and once out the door headed for the bathroom. The milling teenagers outside the bathrooms parted for her, their giggling conversation ceasing. The door handle felt sticky, like the bag of shrimp. Juniper heard a small tinkle, a chain, and felt a slight jerk as she pulled the door. Before she'd fully opened the rickety door, Juniper knew someone was in there but couldn't stop. An irresistible impulse to see the person possessed her, but she didn't really see the woman, only a quick image: mashed potato white thighs pressed together, brown paper towels sticking out between her legs and the toilet seat, short frazzled blonde hair.

"It's occupied!" The woman glared. Juniper was caught in that glare, until shame and humiliation hit, knocking her a step back and releasing the door.

Disoriented by the hoots of the teenagers around her, Juniper slowly turned and started making her way back to the open planks of the pier.

"Somebody's in the bathroom," one of the crew-cut

guys in biker shorts called after her. The others laughed.

Keith handed the torn bag of shrimp back to Juniper. "They give you more at the convenience store up on Middleton."

"I didn't know we were going to need any or else I'd have got some there," she said. She grabbed the shrimp and turned away.

"This is fine. I was just saying, no need to get all worked up about it." Keith gripped his rod underhanded for the cast, and the line sang as it raced out of the open-faced reel. Snapping the face shut, he reeled up the slack.

She pulled one of the cold decapitated shrimp from the bag. The shrimp in their fetal positions seemed the embodiment of defeat. She slipped the hard shell off, ripped off the red legs too, and pushed the pinkish-tinted white meat onto the hook, covering the barb. The wind blew the clear shell and red legs into the ocean. After baiting the other hook, Juniper threw the shrimp, hooks, and lead weight out from the pier. She stood the rod up and rested it in one of the notches carved into the railing. Other things were carved into the wood as well, mostly words: inscrutable words cut too shallow or too long ago to be legible, nonsensical words like "Frund," and initials like "HP" and "DF" that reminded her of the computer she used at the newspaper.

Keith continued to drag the base camp farther and farther out so that they were within listening distance of the King Mackerel fishermen at the end of the pier. At first, he caught only a couple of underweight Spots but finally managed to land a five-pound Sheep's Head. Juniper spent her time pulling up sand sharks. Each one–five in all–wrestled in her grasp, desperately wanting to sink its teeth into her flesh as she struggled to remove the hook with red-handled pliers.

He came back from walking up and down the pier, casting in any empty spot he could find. Juniper grappled with yet another sand shark.

"Could you give me a hand?"

Keith yanked the hook straight out and tossed the six-inch shark over the side. "Ain't this great? I just lost a rig. I think there's something big out there." He wiped his hand on his shorts and ran his fingers through his ruffled hair.

"Yeah, but I think the fish and shrimp smell is getting to me. Can we leave? Just to get a bite to eat?"

"Maybe later. I think I can hook that thing." His fingers moved nimbly tying a new rig on his line. "Besides we walked up and down the beach and went swimming yesterday. That's what you wanted to do."

"You wanted to do that, too."

"Why don't you go grab something to snack on at the tackle shop, and we'll go eat supper a little later?"

She thought she would rather starve than face the Zero girl, the gruff old man, and the bathroom crowd. Hunger hadn't motivated her in the first place; the heat, the need to pee, the smell, the leering rednecks on the opposite side of the pier, and the boredom did.

The sky was empty of thunder clouds, clouds of any kind. Sunshine embraced the pier, warming it like some giant reptile uncoiled from the shore. A fishing boat dragging its nets to the side bobbed gently in the rolling waves. Baiting her second hook, Juniper felt the sway and uncertain jerky bounce of the pier meeting the same waves. The salty breeze picked up, tossing hair and shrimp shells.

Snickering brought her back from the ocean. She was surrounded. The Zero girl stood over the yellow bucket wearing a crooked smile. Two of the arcade girls took up positions opposite her so that Juniper was trapped between them and the bench with the tackle box. The other arcade girl leaned on the rail, blocking Keith's exit–not that he appeared to want to leave. His boyish face broke in a smile.

"What a big, weird fish," the Zero girl said in a huskier voice than Juniper remembered.

"Oh thanks, it's a Sheep's Head."

What is he thanking her for, Juniper thought; the girl didn't say anything to be thanked. Juniper wanted to believe she didn't care, but she couldn't. Like the time a hunched old lady broke in front of her in line at the grocery store–Juniper knew it was nothing; she was in no hurry, but the more she thought how trivial it was, the more anger and shame bubbled in her. She glared at the silver Zero on the girl's shirt.

"I was talking to your older sister here at the bait shop earlier, and I was saying how you looked like a good fisherman. I've been coming here everyday, all week, and you're the best fisherman I've seen."

"Uh, thanks, but–" Keith started, but the girl and her minions walked away back toward the shore, the Zero girl occasionally turning with her black-lipsticked lips pressed together in a grin. Keith shrugged at Juniper. "That's why I like fishing on a pier. You have an audience."

They stood side by side fishing in silence.

S. Craig Renfroe, Jr.

By dark, Juniper had caught nothing else and longed for even a sand shark to break the monotony. Keith had abandoned the shrimp for a small Spot he had caught and cut up for bait. For the last twenty minutes he fought with the thing he thought he'd hooked earlier. She could tell he was still letting it play because she could see the crowd of people who had pulled up their lines to let him through. They were gathered around him three night-lights down on the opposite side of the pier.

She pulled her line up: two empty hooks except for the white slime remnants of the shrimp. The rod fell off the slight indentation she rested it on. She left it on the floor of the pier, took the tackle box off the bench, and sat with her feet kicked up on the railing.

From the cabins lining the shore, sporadic, pathetic fireworks exploded in green and red fizzles, accompanied by lightless pops. Fishing-boat lights out on the edge of the dark sea disappeared and reappeared with the rise and fall of the waves. The cloud-shrouded moon made a shimmering, yellowy-white path on the water, a dancing street.

Juniper thought about how tired she was and about how good it would be to follow the moon road, not have to walk back down the pier past the bathrooms through to the bait shop. The silver path must lead to a place without fishing and without teenagers. A place where she could get some sleep.

The moonbeam path glistened. She leaned on the rail, her body pressed hard against the weathered wood. A dark cloud drifted across the moon cutting a fourth of it from the sky. The path shrank, fleeing from the pier. As it fled,

Juniper climbed the railing. On top, she swung her legs around to face the water and balanced with her hands. A green flip-flop somersaulted its way to the water, made a diminutive splash, and sank.

She was on the other side now, away from the people on the pier. She was on the other side and the moon path was below her, not too far. She could reach it if she'd push off with her feet.

She was flying. Is this what Superman feels like? Her long shirt flapped like a cape. No, she thought, he doesn't fall. She was falling.

She wasn't going to make the moon path; it moved away as she fell. She would never find the other world, and she would never stop falling.

The encasing air vanished, replaced instead with water. Almost solid, she thought, it might've even held her up, and she could've maybe even walked on it–if she walked fast enough–but it parted as she touched it, flowing around her, and she continued to fall. The worse change was the cold, a solid mind-numbing cold, pressing hard all around her. She opened her eyes to darkness. A dim light moved under her, something large and getting larger as she fell and it approached.

The thing, an iridescent white, grew in size and detail into something she could recognize but not name. Within ten feet of it, she realized it was a shrimp, a giant–fifteen-foot-long–shrimp. Its huge segmented tail swirled the water as it came abreast of her. Two ten-foot-long feelers–she thought they looked like whiskers–wrapped around her neck and stopped her descent. The feelers tightened, and she realized she couldn't breathe.

The giant shrimp pulled her to it. Its two stalk eyeballs stared at her; its circular mouth–she wondered at the mouth, not remembering any in smaller shrimp–stood agape with two rigs hanging from it and several rusted hooks around it like bold body piercings. It began to talk, and when it spoke, bubbles floated out of its open hole of a mouth and made vibrations in the water, which were picked up in her ear as unearthly, fluid sounds.

"Matches." It paused as if this were the answer to a very important question.

"Matches," it said in its bubbling language. "You need matches."

She stared back at the eye stalks which were virtually touching her eye lashes. Why would a fifteen-foot shrimp need matches? Did it smoke?

"Matches," it said again and violently shook her. "Matches, matches, matches."

She opened her mouth to answer it or ask it to stop, and the water poured in. She was going to die; she knew this with a certainty colder than the water. She was falling again. Falling deeper and deeper.

She fell through into another place, a lighter place, a place with air. She treaded water, coughing and flicking the plastered hair from her eyes. On the pier, a King Mackerel fisherman talked excitedly to his son–she guessed–and pointed his finger at her. She was a disobedient child who'd gotten into the water when she shouldn't have. The boy took off running. She kicked her feet out, splashing, and threw her arms wildly; if she swam fast enough, she could beat the boy and avoid punishment. The water jostled her, but she jostled it more. A quarter of the way back to the shore, exhausted, she floated on her back and put her arms above her head and gently pushed them down to her sides. From her vantage the few hopeful rods held over the side looked like leafless tree limbs, or maybe tiny legs. Closer in, the waves broke over her; she kept getting water up her nose, coughing and spitting only to get another mouthful of seawater. The salt burned her sinuses, but at last she could touch the soft sand. She wondered when she lost her other flip-flop. The waves still plugged away at her, occasionally knocking her off balance.

On the shore, she saw the steps leading up to the pier. She considered just humming her way down the beach away from the pier, but then the boy appeared before her.

She started up toward the steps, her feet irritably caking with dry sand. She heard the people first, before seeing them, but rose up step by step to face them, an angry mob–or rather a disinterested mob, mostly teenagers looking for excitement. At the head of the group, the gruff old man from the bait shop waited until she stood in front of him next to the bathrooms.

"Can't you read?" he asked. The teens laughed; an older sibling was being punished.

"What?" Juniper looked at him.

He didn't say anything, just pointed. She followed his finger to the blue and white sign listing the rules. The third one said "No diving." His finger jerked away and stabbed in another direction like the air had offended him. There too was a sign, this one smaller: "No diving or jumping from the pier."

She shrugged her wet shoulders; she heard herself dripping. "It was an accident."

"Is the railing broke?" More an accusation than a question.

"No, I just leaned too far over and fell off."

The old man slowly looked her over from head to foot–in a younger, calmer man she'd have taken the look as sexual appraisal. He shook his head and pushed his way through the crowd back toward the bait shop.

She searched the lingering crowd. The girl had to be there laughing and grinning her black-lipstick grin. She'd be ridiculing Juniper's drenched figure to her arcade cronies. All four of them giggling and teetering. A woman with black tresses, too tall and too old, was leaving with one clump of the dispersing crowd. The Zero girl wasn't in the mob, laughing or otherwise. And neither was Keith.

Out past the farthest light, he was bent over the rail, small and alone. His back was a red shell. The two boards of the railing were a part of his body, long encased legs. His arms pitching up and down, the rod pinched in their grasp.

The pier looked every bit like the longest one in North Carolina. Every board a mile, every crack a canyon. She walked past the cutting table over the slippery cold spots that spread from underneath it. She watched the boards' slow progress under her feet and the surging waves below the random spaces, avoiding the heads of nails poking out from old or jarred boards. She glanced up at the fishermen–hardcore devotees this late at night, often shabbily dressed, middle-aged men with varying degrees of facial hair who would lean against the rail, fingers on their lines, and casually follow her passage.

Juniper stood dripping in front of Keith. He looked from her to the rod, its tip bent by the struggling weight on the line. She took the rod from him in his surprise. His deep blue eyes widened as she tossed the rod into the air and off the pier.

JANINE'S DEAD

"Pretend I'm dead," Janine said.

She and I had come to the wood shed out by Grandpa's barn because she wanted to–we could pretend to be frontier people, she'd said. We were supposed to defend the shed from a bandit attack. But the first thing she did was lie down on the ply-wood, which rested on two saw horses for a table.

"I don't like playing this game," I said.

"You're such a baby." Janine giggled her hiccup giggle.

"Shut up," I said.

"If you don't, I'll tell your mom, and she'll wallop you again."

Last week I had refused to go skinny dipping in the pond, and Janine'd told on me.

"Now say nice things. Say how you loved me."

"I don't," I said.

"I'm dead you gotta say you love me."

"Janine's dead, and I love it."

"Cry."

"I don't cry."

"Pretend, dummy. Make noises like you're crying."

I made crying noises.

"Say you hate God because he took me away."

"Mom says I'll go to hell if I say that word."

"What word?"

"That one you said."

"God?"

"Yeah."

"Kiss me."

"Oh gross."

"You have to kiss me. You have to kiss dead people."

"I didn't kiss Grandma."

"Not old dead people."

"You're not dead," I said.

"I could be. Kiss me."

"I have to go home."

"I'm telling."

I could still feel the beating I got when Janine lied to Mom and said I went swimming naked. Mom had a switch she'd cut from a thorn bush. So I leaned over Janine like in a Disney movie. Janine's breathe smelled like peanut butter and ketchup but her hair like oranges. I could see her eyeballs peeking out from under their scrunched-up lids, and as I got closer, I thought I could hear her heart beat, beat, beat. I puckered my lips, hovering above her, half an inch.

How do you do it, I wondered; do you just touch her lips?

Do you suck on them?

Some of the boys at school spat in girls' mouths and called it frenching. Down, I thought, but my head wouldn't move; it refused, Janine shifting impatiently.

I lined up our lips, closed my eyes, and let gravity pull my head the rest of the way–not as wet as I'd thought, but soft. It made me think of pillows, the down pillows on Grandpa's bed. When Janine's lips began to move, squirm, I opened my eyes, hers already wide open, sparkling. I pulled away. She started her hiccup giggle, but it broke into a deep laugh.

I spat on the ground and ran home.

Mom was pushing a rolling pin over wet flour to make dumplings. I asked her if Janine would ever die. Mom said yes. I asked her if Janine would ever get married one day. Mom said yes. Then she said I was too young to worry about marriage and death. And so I went out looking for Janine.

MISTLETOE HUNT

Stub celebrated his eighty-second birthday a week before Christmas, a late December birthday, "a child close to Christ" his mama always said, and he should be getting closer to Christ as old as he was, but he didn't feel it. He'd been too bad a person: left his family those seven years to wander, took up with Bell–long dead–and only came back to Ellie out of habit. But now those seven years didn't seem all that much, not with all the others stacked beside. The days collected like dust.

He stood up from the breakfast table, amazed to hear no creak or pop.

"What you doing?" Ellie asked.

"I'm going to get some mistletoe."

"Why?"

"We always get mistletoe."

"We haven't got any in years. The kids is all gone and none of them coming this year. Except Cheryl might make it down New Years."

"I'm getting some."

He went out to the porch, put on his shoes, his boots over them, his orange hunting hat with the fuzzy ear flaps, his blue jean jacket under the down ski coat, and his yellow work gloves, the ones with the tips cut out; he felt like a damn rainbow. The shotgun rested behind the door to the hall. He picked it up and breached the single barrel, let it rest in the crook of his arm, checked in the laundry cupboard and found the box of shells, took a few and put one in the barrel. He fingered the safety off and then back on.

Outside, Stub stopped for a minute to watch his cloudy breath spiral away from him. Ear flaps down, he held the shotgun like an ax over his shoulder with the barrel resting on his neck. The woods lay over beyond the dormant fields, an hour's walk, though he could remember when it took him half that.

The door slammed. He turned to see Ellie coming toward him, bundled in what he called her "Eskimo parka." He went on, knowing she'd catch up.

They slowed down in the woods, dodging briars, stepping over dead logs, pushing aside low limbs. Stub, who hadn't been to the back of his place in over a year, shook his head at the barbed wire fence, its broken strands, leaning posts. It was all falling down. That's what he hated about the farm: the fight and the inevitable collapse. Even when he was away, asleep in Bell's arms, he'd dreamed about the work that needed to be done. With every completed task, you only created two more that needed doing. Then, that wasn't his problem, anymore, his fields rented, his cows tended by his nephew.

"We'll have to fix the fence."

"Why?" Ellie asked.

"Needs fixing."

"Nothing to keep in anymore."

"Why'd you come along?" Stub asked.

"We used to go together."

He nodded, partly ducking a bent maple branch. "Guess so."

A creek twisted out of a patch of oaks, their roots stretching across to the other side, natural bridges. The creek's creeping flow was dappled from the winter sun's rays peeking through the branches.

"Where are we going?" Ellie asked.

"The trees on down are thicker with it."

Ellie made a show of looking up at the green bunches cropping out of the tops of the oaks. Stub followed her gaze up. The ground beneath his feet gave way; he'd gotten too close to the bank. To not fall headfirst, Stub gave a little leap, pushing off from the dirt avalanche. He landed in the cold slow muck of the stream and brought the shotgun out in front of him in both hands, balancing with it like he was a tight-rope walker. The water was just deep enough to make it over the lip of his boots. He hooted at the wet cold sipping in.

Ellie carefully edged to the side. "Look at you."

Stub stood a couple feet from the bank; his boots were filling and drops of water were splattered up on his overalls. He trudged toward the creek-side, got up to a point where he started slipping back into the water, the bank too steep and slick for him to climb out. He grabbed a small root dangling and managed to pull it out before he pulled himself up. The cold in his feet made it hard for him to think; he considered the bank like a mountaineer laying plans.

"Here take a hold of this." Stub reached the shotgun toward Ellie.

"Don't you point that gun at me."

"The safety's on."

"I don't care. Don't point that thing at me."

Stub swung the barrel around to face him and took the end of it. "Get the stock."

Ellie crept closer to the gun and touched the dark wood stock with the tips of her fingers, then let it rest on the palm of her hand.

"Now pull me up."

"You want me to pull you up? You're crazy."

"Try."

Stub tugged on the shotgun and splashed backward as it came out of Ellie's hands.

Steady again, he grabbed the shotgun by the stock and took a moment to reach in his back pocket for his pouch. The tinfoil mouth unfolded; he gingerly placed a pinch of Redman Select tobacco in-between his lip and gum.

Ellie shook her head.

"I'm too old to quit."

"You're also too old to be wading in a creek."

They stared at each other. Stub thought about Ellie as a young girl in Sunday school making faces at him, squinting her eyes and shooting her tongue out like a lizard. Bell had made faces at him in the morning when she thought he was asleep.

"I'm going to get help," Ellie said.

"You're leaving me?" Stub asked.

"It'll just be for a minute."

"Two hours."

"I can't get you out. I'll get James."

"The wolves will get me."

Ellie didn't move but fidgeted with the hem of her parka. Stub looked around, up and down the creek, and noticed the broken limb lying over the bank, the thinning branches resting in the brown water. He pointed, but Ellie was already headed toward it. She moved the limb by rowing the part in the water up toward him and then picking up her end and walking down the creek: row, walk, row. With the limb in reach, Stub passed her the shotgun and holding onto the limb for support and leverage, worked his way up the bank, the scaly bark breaking off in his hands and scattering to the creek below. Sitting back away from the crumbled edge, Stub emptied the water from his boots.

Ellie handed him the shotgun, and he used it to get to his feet. Gun over his shoulder, he squeaked deeper into the woods.

"Where are you going?"

"I'm going to get some mistletoe."

"You'll catch death."

"Little water never hurt anybody." He spit out a dark glob of tobacco juice.

"Stubborn." Ellie said it like a curse.

The clumps of green mistletoe in the tree turned a barren winter into a faux spring. Stub raised the gun–its weight a bit resistant to the idea–tried to match the center of a bunch with the hairs of the sight but couldn't stop shaking, pulled the trigger. Nothing. He'd left the safety on. It took another minute to steady himself enough to aim, again. He was circling the mistletoe, the gun jumping the more he tried to be still. Frustrated, he shot. Instantaneously, he heard the crack, the thunder of the explosion, and felt the kick of the shotgun in his shoulder, which made a nice balance to the numbness in his feet.

He watched for falling green, but nothing fell. How could he miss with a shotgun, he thought, a shotgun. He breached the barrel and tossed the spent shell to the ground.

"Here," Ellie said, "Brace the gun up against the trunk of this tree."

Gun reloaded, Stub raised it, freehanded, for the second shot. The shaking was worse; he'd have to watch to see if he shook the gun in the direction of the mistletoe. He pulled the trigger. A couple twigs from the oak cart-wheeled through the air to the leaf-covered ground. Stub spit.

"It's higher," Ellie said.

Stub waited for the fall, the rain. If he didn't blow that green off the tree, he'd be back with his chainsaw.

"How many shells you bring?"

"Three."

Stub jammed the shell into place. Focus, he thought, it's all mental, and for now he still had that. He aimed at a limb closer but with fewer groups. Instead of resting the barrel in his palm, he laid it on his arm and slid the gun up slowly, up to the low limb. One, two, three, fire.

A clump of mistletoe exploded into a confetti of green, fluttering down. Stub walked over to the pieces, the tiny shreds of mistletoe. He hadn't hit the base, but the ends, the shot tearing them to bits. Even the few whole leaves were berry-less. Stub kicked at the ground, disturbing the packed oak leaves from autumn, and headed home, past Ellie.

They walked back in silence, the only sound coming from Stub's occasional stops to spit. Stub looked again at the leaning fence, the broken strands. Used to, he thought, things never went without doing. But now, they'd be drowned in the unpainted, unplowed, unwatered, unnailed, undusted details of their lives. Once when their days consisted of dawn rises and chores till noon and dinners of fat back and okra and more work and a fried chicken, turnip green supper, they said they were happy. Now they slept to nine, walked the yard, got the mail, ate a white okra dinner without cornbread–no more green foods because they interfered with the blood thinners–napped, a nap forgodsake, watched the inane babble on TV, ate a low-sodium supper, walked the yard, slept, nothing else. He spat the last of the chew to the cold ground.

Back in the house, Stub changed out of his wet clothes–the boots made a sucking sound as he pulled them off. In his thermal underwear, he wandered to the living room where he sat in front of the gas stove. His feet began to hurt as they warmed up. He idly wondered if it was frostbite.

Ellie came out of the kitchen, an angel's food cake with butterscotch icing held in front of her, an offering. On the top, in the very center, were two green leaves with a pristine white berry in the middle, whole except a tiny nick on the right leaf, a mark that by comparison proved the whole's perfection. She must've picked it up when he walked off.

"You know," Stub said, "Mistletoe berries are poisonous."

"We'll split it then." She took off the leaves and berry, setting it on the coffee table, and cut two pieces of the cake. She gave Stub the bigger one.

Whether he deserved it or not, it'll be like this to the end, Stub thought.

S. Craig Renfroe, Jr.

BIOPSY DOPPELGANGER

One day this thing showed up on my lip. I thought it might be a pimple or a boil, so I kept squeezing it, but it wouldn't pop and it didn't hurt. I hazarded it was herpes, but it didn't ooze anything gross. Wart, perhaps? I couldn't remember biting my lip. I ignored it. That worked until it started to get bigger. And it began bleeding. Blood in the shower. Blood on the rim of my cups. Bloody little squares of toilet tissue scattered around my bathroom, as if I were shaving with a butcher's knife. People started to notice. They had only one line, like a Greek chorus: "You should get that looked at." I ignored them. Then, after the crusty scab I'd been playing with finally fell off and revealed a small eye, a baby's eye, I decided to go to the doctor.

"You have a cyst," he said.

"What the hell is a cyst?"

"An abnormal membranous sac."

"It's an eye. Doesn't it look like an eye?"

He looked at it. "It's a cyst."

"A cyst that looks like an eye?"

"It'll have to be removed. Here, apply some Triple Antibiotic Ointment to it for two weeks and don't take any aspirin."

"Will that make it go away?"

"No, come back in two weeks, and we'll take care of it."

"I don't like the sound of that?"

"We'll cut it out."

"I like the sound of that even less."

As the first week went by the eye enlarged, became adult-sized. And as I typed in a fidgeting couple's tax return for an H&R Rapid Refund, something gave way on my lip. It'd fallen off, I thought, relieved, but a quick finger check found the familiar lump–though not so familiar. The fidgeting couple had been valiantly attempting to avoid staring at it and avoid the appearance of straining to do so, but when the lump moved they leapt out of their seats. Refund or not, they were gone. Strangers reacted that way, looking or conspicuously not looking. Friends and family downplayed it: "Not bad," "Barely noticeable," "You'd have to tell me it's there." All of which, though couched in the intentions of reassurance, basically amounted to: "Enough about you." Which taught me how terribly lonely dying was going to be.

In the bathroom mirror, I marveled at the disappearance of the eye. Replaced with a pinkish membrane. I tapped it. The new skin slid back, with a sickening mucus sucking sound, into my lip to expose the eye. Then, the flap slipped back out. It'd grown an eyelid.

Most everyone had abandoned me, except Jill-Ann. The fair-weather friends took rain checks, but Jill-Ann was a storm chaser. "Can I go to the doctor with you?" she'd ask. Then, she started insisting. I needed caring for. She brought me casseroles, though the only thing I was doing was applying Triple Antibiotic Ointment and not taking aspirin.

"You know I had surgery once," Jill-Ann said.

"Fascinating."

"I understand what you're going through."

"Am I in surgery?"

"The bump just popped out."

Sure enough, in the bathroom mirror, I saw that it'd broken free of the lip, hanging out with a mass below it. Was that a nose?

I almost got fired the next day. I got angry and accused my boss of firing me because of the extra nose. She said it was because I hadn't filled out any returns in the past few days. It was hard to prepare taxes for people who ran away. She settled on letting me fill in the drop offs in the back room. Alone with a tiny desk and surrounded by the wide array of IRS forms, I heard a terrible whistling noise. I pulled out the pocket mirror I kept on me. The nose had cleared a hole and begun breathing. You could make out a small nostril. I pinched it shut. The eyelid flew open and the brown iris, like my own, stared at me in the makeup mirror. It squinted and glared. It didn't like that one bit. Finally tired, I let go. The whispery wheezing noise returned and the eye shut.

The nurse read something written in pencil on my folder. "And you have an allergy to basilhefflinne."

"What?"

"It causes you diarrhea."

"No. No, I've never even heard of that. What is it? Basil?"

"It's an antibiotic."

"I've never taken it. Never."

She looked doubtful. "Are you taking any medications now?"

"Why is that written on my folder?"

"I'll check on it."

She finished her questionnaire and conducted me into the operating room, an operating table covered in a white cloth. She asked me to wash the cyst. I scrubbed the hell out of the closed eyelid hoping in this last ditch effort it would fall off. But I only managed to get water down the nostril and have to hear it sniff loudly.

I got on the table as ordered and was hooked up to a machine while the doctor washed up. I heard the machine go wild. "Relax, relax," the nurse said. I tried to relax. The doctor smiled over me and asked for me to open as wide as I could. Then, the bastard dropped a metal box in my mouth that held it that way. He asked the nurse for an instrument, then apologized for the needle, but said I wouldn't feel it for long. He was right. Except I could feel something, like he was filling my lip full of cement. My lip must be huge. Enormous. Then, he threw a towel over my face–to keep the light out of my eyes, he said. The nurse turned on Motown's greatest hits. I thought I could smell a scented candle. I listened to the ABC song trying to relax, wondering when he would start already. But the next instant, I felt a warm fluid dribbling down my chin. I was bleeding. Christ, I was bleeding, and I didn't feel a thing. Surgery wasn't so bad. I was rather enjoying it.

From my lip I heard, "Agggrrhrhheeeee. Aheeeee. Heeee. Heeey. Hey."

"It goes deeper than I thought," the doctor said. "Sarah, go get an anesthesiologist."

I tried to talk, but the contraption didn't allow it. I moaned.

"Nothing to worry about."

"Worrrry," someone else said, a voice all liquid. "Ouuuut."

"Nothing to worry about."

"Ouuuuuuuut. Leeeet."

"Nothing to worry about."

I was worried. But the nurse came back with another voice–this one not so scary. The new voice counted backwards, and I wasn't anything.

I woke to the nurse humming "I Will Survive," while she cleaned something in the sink. My face felt empty. "Am." Speaking nearly tore my lip apart.

"Settle down, dear. Had a scare there. But it went great. Just great. Doctor be back in a minute to finish up with you."

The doctor came with a slip of paper. He took a second to admire his handiwork on my face. "Yes, the stitches should heal nicely. Try not to talk too much for a few days though. Or chew. And don't smile."

I could do that last one. I don't smile.

"Okay, here's your prescription for the hydrocodone and antibiotic–and don't worry it's not basilhefflinne."

"Wha?"

"You know, your gas problem."

"I've neva takun tha. Neva."

"Hm. Maybe there's two of you. A name mix up."

"Two?"

"No talking, champ. Now, get some rest. Biopsy'll be in, in a week."

A week passed with my friends and family coming

out of their storm cellars. "Looks great." "Can't tell a thing." "Wouldn't've noticed if you didn't tell me." But I had eyes–though only two now–and I could see the Frankenstein stitches cris-crossing their way down my swollen lip, down to my chin. I got high off the hydrocodone and forgot about it all until:

"Your cyst has been misplaced," the doctor said.

"Escaped?"

"But we have the report, and it's not good. It could be growing."

"Did you feed it?"

"One more bit of bad news. It's malignant."

"Well, I could've told you that." I had never liked how that eye squinted.

And just as suddenly as they came, my friends and family were once again gone. Except Jill-Ann. She grew positively excited at the prospects of seeing me through this one. She came over so often, she began talking about moving in.

"I understand." She was putting ointment over my stitches to keep them moist. She had also brought some vitamin E to prevent scarring. "You're scared."

"No, I'm not." I've never been scared. I learned when I was a little tyke that you can't control what life gives you; you can only control your response to it. And my response has always been a gentle indifference. No fear, no regret.

"It's okay we all get scared. Can I make you some dumplings?"

"You can get the hell out."

"But dumplings are soft so you won't have to chew much."

"I'll chew gum if I want. Just go away."

She stayed and made dumplings. After we'd finished eating and she'd done the dishes, I threw her out. I didn't need her pity.

A month went away and so did my stitches and scars–thanks to the vitamin E, I guess. I had gotten a job with an actuary. I could find no Life Expectancy Table with my condition on it.

My grandma called from the Home and said she was glad to see me but wanted to know why I had kept asking her all those questions. Naturally, I thought the old woman had finally gone senile. But two days later I got a message from Jill-Ann saying she loved the flowers. I called her and told her they weren't from me.

"You said you'd say that."

"No, I didn't."

"And you said it meant that you love me."

"Go to hell."

Someone was playing terrible tricks on me, and though I immediately knew who, I tried to deny it. If that biopsied mess had continued to grow at the rate it had on my face, it'd be a full-grown person soon enough. The eye looked like me, and I fathered the thing, so it must resemble me. Enough at least to fool an Alzheimer-addled grandmother and a love-starved woman. It didn't fool me.

People think some people just up and disappear. That even certain celebrities disappear. Take Ambrose Bierce for instance. Famous writer. Inflamer of passions. Then one day vanishes into Mexico. Victim of Pancho Villa, some say. But now I know the truth. It's all there between the lines, on the Internet. Bierce had his own doppelganger chopped off, though it was in a back-alley Mexican medical bar–he couldn't afford the scandal in the States. But like me, it was too late. His other survived. Why didn't Bierce come back? Same reason Amelia Earhart, Richey Edwards, and Glenn Miller didn't, not to mention hundreds of nobodies. There's a thousand different places to focus blame and anger in this terrible world, but when it comes down to it, we're all fighting ourselves. And sometimes, that other self wins. And once it does, it has other plans. Why wouldn't the doppelganger return to Bierce's life? What could it offer him? He had fought his way out for a reason, and that reason wasn't to be consumed back into the leftover trappings of the old Bierce but to have his own life. Partly, I sympathize with the other me; what kind of loneliness is it to only be the flip side of someone else? But also, I fully intend on kicking my ass.

The doctor calls again.

"Have you found him? The biopsy," I ask.

"No, we can't find it. Some kind of mix up." He clears his throat, sounding sick. "We have to talk. About your treatments. You'll experience changes in your body. You won't feel like yourself."

"No, thanks. There's too much of that going around."

Lately, I've been having to ask myself would I do that, would Me-me do that or would Me-not-me do that? Would I do that because Me-not-me wouldn't expect it? Would I do it to spite Me-not-me? I have this fear of becoming my other. He's making me not act like myself out of fear of giving Me-not-me a predictable target. Maybe I'm being paranoid. Why does the other me have to be out to get me? People all the time hear that they have look-alikes, twins, doppelgangers walking around. "I saw your spitting image down at the Wal-mart." But even that kills you a little. The thought that someone else has something of yours, some appearance, some way about him, some genetic code, lessens your individuality. My double can't let me go on living, not and feel anything but inferior, copy that he is.

Two brown eyes stare at me from the mirror. I press my lip and feel the hard scar tissue underneath, unseen but there. I am me.

There's a knock on the bathroom door. "Are you okay?" I'd forgotten Jill-Ann had come over with a casserole and had yet to leave though we'd already finished eating. I open the door on her. She's heavy and limpid, dazzlingly normal in her self-assured goodness, never suspecting everyone hates her.

"Get out of my way."

"I want to take care of you."

"Take care of my laundry."

"I know you said that if I loved you, I would leave you in peace. Give you your space, but please, I want to be with you. I can help you through this."

I would never say those things. Certainly not to her. It must have been the other me.

"I see I'm hurting you," she says. "I'll go to save you any more pain."

She stands leaning, swaying toward me slightly, waiting in my silence for me to contradict her, to grab her in my arms. I put my hands in my pockets. She gathers her Tupperware and leaves. The doppleganger accomplished what I couldn't. Why did Jill-Ann choose now to start listening to me?

When I get to work the next day, my desk has been cleaned off. All my work and folders gone, my smiley-face coffee cup missing, my little name plate nowhere to be seen. I open the top drawer and find it empty but for a rainbow packet of post-its. My supervisor tells me I quit and took my things away. He can't seem to look me in the eye. I try to apologize, but he apologizes for my apology, standing and leading me from his office, from his sight.

I sit in the back of my apartment on the bed. I've got a piece of notebook paper and a phone book to write on. So far I have: "Dear." I can't seem to follow that with anything. Or anyone, rather. I guess I'm just waiting. How long is it till I hear the door? How would he have gotten in? Would the landlord give him the spare key? Did I even lock it?

He stands in the hallway like a movie star. He's a handsome bastard. Why didn't I ever cut my hair that way? Where did he buy that suit? I wish that'd always been me.

"It's time," he says. His voice is calm and low.

"All right. I'm a man. I can take it." But I can't; I start to cry.

IN THE DARK

Leslie took her baths in the dark. That's what her roommates told me anyway. She didn't want to see herself naked, they said. How do you know? I said. I think they came to that conclusion on their own; surely, Leslie didn't come out and say I don't like seeing myself naked. She always waited till dark to take a bath, they said, and there was never any light under the door; besides, Colette walked in on her one night. Don't you think that's weird? they said. No, I don't think she was weird at all, I said. You don't know, they said; you ran off when it happened. That sounds weird to us, they said. Colette thinks you killed her, they said. Maybe I did, I said.

They told me all this after Leslie's death. We were on the roof of the flat at 83 Queensway in London. We'd all been drinking: they wine, me vodka and 7-up. The December wind was cold, but we didn't feel it. The golden Christmas lights shone three blocks down at Whitley's department store. I marveled at the empty street below; at only 2:00 a.m., the city slept as if dead. Some cosmopolitan capital this was.

I'd first met Leslie at night. I was just going to the last showing of *Even Cowgirls Get the Blues,* which turned out to be a horrid movie with only one redeeming feature: a cameo by William S. Burroughs, who accurately assessed the situation as "ominous." She sat on the padded bench in the lobby of Cinema 8. I'd seen her before at Lossdor, a private college we both attended, but it took a minute to recognize her that night because her hair was newly dyed a stark white blonde.

We made our awkward introductions. She'd seen me working in the library and writing in the computer lab at Lossdor. She noticed I was quiet like her. I asked her if she was waiting for someone.

"No, I work here. I'm the projectionist."

You're as high up in the movie business as you can get, I said. She laughed.

"I like it. You don't have to deal with people. The projection booth is a nice retreat. It's a zen sort of place."

You look different with your new hair, I said.

"This is my real hair, my natural color. I was dying it brown but decided it wasn't me. Strange to get up in the morning and not recognize yourself."

She had a nervous tic of pushing her hair behind her small, earringless ears, only for it to fall free with one tilt of her head and her to push it back. She wore a dark wool sweater with long sleeves that slipped over her hands and had holes where her thumbs poked through. When not playing with her hair, she'd rub her sweater-covered hands together like she was starting a fire.

In the theater, I sat in the middle–far enough from the back to have a good view of the projectionist's window. I wanted to catch a glimpse of Leslie turning on the movie. Her thumbs gripping knobs through her thick sweater sleeves, the toes of her black sneakers crumpling as she stands on her tip-toes to tug on a piece of reluctant film, the white tips of her hair dribbling over her shoulder and coalescing in the swell of her breasts. Maybe I'd wave.

But when the lights dimmed and the brilliant light poured out of the booth, Leslie was nowhere in sight. How do they turn those movies on? Doesn't she have to be up there looking through the window? Wouldn't her face show in the glow of the projector bulb?

Maybe I should ask her if she wants to get some coffee at the Waffle House after work, I thought. She's a rock, a mysterious stone. But I could hear her excuses: I have to work tomorrow, I have a lot of studying to do, I'm awfully tired but thanks.

The next year, in the Charlotte-Douglas International Airport, running to my gate with black leather carry-on and parents in tow, I saw her at the terminal, alone in an orange-cushioned chair, pushing her hair behind her ears. We were all there for Lossdor-in-London, a semester long sojourn to England complete with British dons and European travel. I didn't think about her too much during the three tiring flights that took us to Heathrow.

The next month we spent acclimating to a culture so similar to our own that the minor differences were jarring. The loo–the bathroom, a flat–an apartment, the BBC–the only damn thing on TV, the tube–the intricate subway system, fish and chips–fast food, a pub–a cool bar, pissed–drunk. Baffling accents, more Pakistanis than Brits, lectures (classes) with only one paper to determine our grade. The city itself a string of sensual explosions we were unprepared for. People everywhere, crowding and begging in the streets, shoving in the tube, laughing in the pubs.

At first, we stayed mostly in the flats: two for guys and three above for girls. We played chess and made fun of the stupid things on TV. I started the chess playing, bought a marble board (no store sold those in Lossdor) which ended up in the common room scuffed from countless pawns marching to their doom.

Leslie was the only girl who played chess. In fact, one of the only two girls I'd ever known who played chess at all. The other was Karen Cox, a girl from my high school. She also dyed her hair, but black to match all her clothes. She was the only girl in the chess club and my only real competition. I'd asked Karen to the prom. No, I don't think so, she'd said; I'm not going. She went with a friend of mine. They came in drunk and without formal wear and got kicked out for pushing over the punch bowl.

As a convoluted British movie about murder with blunt objects played in the background, I beat Leslie at another game, my queen cornering her defenseless king. She demanded another game. "Your luck's exhausted," she said. She always refused to give up unless she won or was beaten in five consecutive games. And then she'd curse; while I reserved my battery of foul language for male opponents, she felt free to insult my mother, manhood, and future progeny.

While we played, I watched her moves: Pawn to Queen Four, Knight to King's Bishop Three, Queen to King Two. The pieces moving themselves, no fingers, no hand, no arm, no face. But in class as our British History professor droned on about the English monarchy, all I could see was her hair, the way it slipped off her crooked "s" ear. I imagined her tapping her thin finger with its grey-painted nail on my captured knight, looking at my furrows of deep concentration and smiling.

Once during a class trip, Leslie sat at the ferry's window and looked out except when for some reason she turned to me. She stared at me for a full minute, not turning away, not blinking, not saying anything, only staring; then she turned back to the spray-covered window. I imagined the two of us on the windblown deck, her white-blonde hair dancing madly. I'd tuck a bunch of chorus-line hairs behind her ear and tell her how unearthly she had looked that first time in the glow of the movie projector. We'd stay on deck until the chill huddled us together, then go into the lounge for a drink of wine and a quick game before arriving at Normandy.

In addition to playing chess and ridiculing the British soap operas set in Australia, the group drank. Leslie'd never go with us to the pubs though. "I'll come later, reading to do." But she never showed. She held no clean and straight precept that I knew. She was a drinker. Though I couldn't remember seeing her with a glass in hand, I could see her lips meeting the chilled glass, the golden cider rising and falling in her throat. Come to think of it, we'd attended countless group dinners, breakfasts, and such, but I couldn't remember her eating, but I imagined the way she'd pick at her food or the way she'd hold her mouth while she chewed: her fork cutting triangular portions of shepherd's pie, small lumps appearing and disappearing in the sides of her marble cheeks.

She didn't eat at Pot Luck that night. She sat in silence with us at a circular table of dark wood. Later, the police asked her roommates if Leslie said anything about suicide or feeling depressed over dinner. No, they said, but we wouldn't put it past her. We think that's what probably happened, they said. To me they said this; to the police, they said simply, no.

After dinner, her roommates left to go down to Piccadilly Circus. Leslie headed back in my incidental company. We talked hesitantly of what we each thought of London on our way to the tube station. Have you done everything you want to do, I asked.

"All except going to Dover. I have to see Dover," she said.

What's so special about Dover, I asked.

"The white cliffs of Dover. Sheer cliffs dropping off the side of towering mountains. The white glare blinding you like heaven. Though I've never been, I know it's beautiful, the kind of beauty where you can't breathe from looking at it," she said. She seemed embarrassed for having said so much.

On the train she took a book–*The Secret History*, I think–out of her pocket and proceeded to read, pushing hair behind her ears ceaselessly.

Near the Bayswater stop, I stood up. "Back home," I said.

"No, I think I'm going to stay on a little longer. I like to ride the entire circuit. Read some. Watch the people."

"Okay," I said. I'd hoped to play her in chess when we got back, and I'd planned to watch her that time.

The train slowed coming into the station. What would she do if I asked her to go to Dover. To spend the weekend walking under and on those white cliffs. I stood five feet away from her, holding onto one of the poles in the middle of the car. I wanted to take her chess-piece hands; I turned to her. See you later, I said. She made no reply.

The walk through the station to the outside world was exhausting. I didn't notice anyone's face or their clothes, not even their smell–so strong in the overheated bowels of cold London. The city had become endless streams of humanity where faces ran together, becoming a thing to struggle with and against, like rats in a mad scientist's maze. The walk to the flat was cold and wet. The overhead bulb above our flat entrance had burnt out, so the key had to be fit into the lock by feel. Even in the dark, I got the key in on the first try.

We played chess and drank that night. I won a lot; I don't know against whom. I stayed in my chair until they gave up, and then I went to bed.

The next morning, early, Dr. Carnes gathered everyone in her flat. As the program director she often called us together for news from Lossdor or explanations of travel plans or words of warning. This time a policeman–a bobby, looking clownish in his big hat–and a woman, who, I suppose, was some kind of therapist, were there. Last night, your classmate Leslie Wooten was tragically killed, they said. Apparently, she had gone to Harrod's or had at any rate ended up at that tube station, they said. It gets very crowded at the Harrod's stop, especially this time of year, they said. So crowded that Leslie was accidently knocked off onto the tracks, they said. It happens a lot, we're afraid; more than you'd think, they said. You were the last one here to see her, they said. Did she say anything? they said. I have to go to the bathroom, I said. We understand, they said.

I left the flats and took the tube to Victoria station. I bought a rail ticket to Dover. The trip didn't last long; I didn't realize I was there until I was paying for a room in a white-washed bed-and-breakfast called the Dover House.

I turned on all the lights and took a long shower in the hard British water. How did she die, I wondered. They hadn't said anything about that. Was she run over by the train? Were the tracks electrified? Did she just break her neck from the fall?

I changed back into the clothes I'd worn: a black and white sweater, a pair of blue jeans, and a pair of hiking boots. I hadn't thought to bring anything else with me.

The walk to the shore wasn't what I expected. The cliffs weren't like she said. The mountains weren't that big and the cliffs not that steep or white–more beige really, dull, not glinting. Not breathtaking, like she said.

PROJECT CASANOVA

She stood across the white, sanitized bed, impatiently waiting to have sex with me. Her head cocked to the side, her hair dyed raven black, hanging in her right eye–her good eye, I supposed, seeing as how her left one was giving me the evil eye. She had a certain way about her, like a bee sting. She canted her hips to and fro, shifting her weight from one foot to the other. Arcanely attractive, her deep pale skin and exaggerated curves shaped a white t-shirt and a pair of red panties. With her daddy-longleg fingers, she twisted a silver thumb ring. I felt a headache coming on.

"You want to make out a little first?" I asked.

"No. I want to get this over with."

"What was your name again?"

"Griffin."

"Like the mythic beast with the head of an eagle, the body of a lion and the tail of a scorpion, right?"

"I have a dentist appointment. Let's get started."

"I thought we could talk. How about we go see a movie and come back next week?"

"We're getting paid."

"Coffee?"

"No. We're just having sex. That's it." She tilted her head the other way; her eyes were equally evil. "Now!"

There was no reasoning with her.

I glanced nervously up at the observation platform where two men, one with glasses and one without, and one woman, who looked male except for the bulge of her chest, all garbed in white lab coats, watched.

"What's your sign?" I asked. As I spoke, I could already see that was a mistake.

She moved to the right. I moved to the left.

"I was thinking that perhaps by 'copulation' they might actually be referring to a sort of capitulation where we could come together in a verbal manner and get to know each other."

She started slowly circling the bed.

"Then maybe move on to some heavy petting. I mean I signed up for next week, right? How about you? I mean we could do this as an ongoing thing."

She jumped, straight over the bed, had a hold of my white undershirt, and dragged me on top of her, half on and half off. We struggled. It was like wrestling, the high school kind, not that fake professional stuff. I had to admit she was strong, but finally I managed to pull out of the undershirt, leaving her on the bed twisting it in her hands like she'd strangle me with it.

The white coats were scribbling away.

"You big tough guys, signing up to get laid. Then when you get in here and have a little pressure you just fold, like when somebody stands beside you at a urinal and you can't pee."

How'd she know about that, I wondered.

She turned to the lab people and held up her hands as if in defeat, as if she couldn't do anything else with me. I thought that very condescending. Definitely not my type.

After I got my money–they were very understanding–I went to Barnes & Noble, read some of *The Year's Best*

Erotica, and glanced through the latest *Movieline* for the actress layout–I was too embarrassed to flip through *Playboy*. I didn't leave until they asked me to, around midnight, an hour after they closed; the key was to hide in the kid's section. I'd brought an Anais Nin book back there for company. On the way to my one-room apartment, I thought about my situation. I kept in touch with my friends from college, and they stayed as perennially dateless as I, except for Henson, but then he slept with high school girls. Something had gone wrong; I was scared, scared of what exactly I didn't know: sexual harassment? feminism? marriage? living together? commitment? talk shows? Maybe all of it.

Sure I had friends that stumbled into relationships. Hubert dated a Brazilian till she went back to Brazil. Cliffton was dating a PhD candidate in African Lit Studies till she smoked a formaldehyde-laced joint and went permanently psychotic. Geoffrey was once engaged, but his fiancée turned Wiccan and shacked up with an herbalist, and then she sued Geoffrey for half the cost of her wedding dress. Winston got a woman over the Internet who lived in Seattle, and though he called it electronic dating, I called it pathetic. And I knew married couples, but they seemed to have acquired the status as a disease, a disease to which I was apparently immune.

My last relationship ended when I dropped by Betty's apartment and her roommate Amber answered but pretended not to know me. She kept it up until I told her I knew for a fact she collected her belly button lint in a Band-Aid box, and I didn't mind letting others know. She said Betty moved, planned to move for a long time and decided not to tell me. Figured she needed a clean break.

My lesbian neighbors were happily spooning on the fold-out couch in the glow of an iridescent sit-com. They had the charitable habit of leaving their blinds up. I once saw one of them naked and caught glimpses of kissing–not that I went out of my way to look, naturally. The one who lived there first wasn't always a lesbian. She had a boyfriend for a while, but she was apparently too religious for him. Late at night, she would yell "Oh God! Oh God! Oh God!" I could hear it through the wall, and it went on for hours after I was done and could only stare at the ceiling appreciating her religious ecstasy.

My other neighbor had a shower fetish. I could hear him talking women into the shower: "Come on baby; it's great with water." Night and day, I'd hear the rumble through the wall, water striking the plastic. And then the pounding. He took an average of five showers a day. Some of them alone.

The first thing I looked at coming through my door was the beady red light of my answering machine. I had a message, my existence validated. But then it turned out to be Mom calling to tell me Grandpa was back in the hospital. He'd been practicing at dying for two years now, ever since Grandma died from heart failure. They were married for sixty-eight years. Their marriage was like God to me–I couldn't get my mind around it.

There was fuzz all over the place again. My black leather recliner bled yellow fuzz. Apparently, a spring was loose in the back, and every time I reclined, it ate away at the stuffing. If it kept losing fuzz like that, it'd be dead soon.

I swept up the fuzz and went to bed.

I had a dream about the girl from the sex experiment, Griffin, but I forgot it. I made a habit of forgetting my dreams because dreams can never come true; unless, of course, you don't remember them, then you won't know any better. It was all part of my complicated life philosophy, the main part of which had to do with situational ethics: no rules, just questions.

Of late my question was: what would Casanova do? It was the in-thing. A rock magazine had just come out with the question: what would Journey do? But Journey was a bunch of pansies. And there was my mother's insistent advice to always think: what would Jesus do? I, however, knew what Jesus would do and didn't think it would get me very far.

I went through my morning routine. Another day of accounts payable. Another day of chit-chat with the overweight dead-ends who–based on the way they talked–were all married to the same kind of insufferable woman.

That afternoon in Barnes & Noble, I saw Griffin again. She was in the Computer Science section. I passed her on my way to put back the copy of De Sade's *Justine* I'd been perusing, but she didn't notice me–too engrossed in a thick volume on some computer language.

And that was where it would have ended, had I not followed her. At first, I felt bad. I was stalking her. I was a stalker. I was one of those guys that don't wash their hair for weeks and wear black knit hats and watch Japanese animé and pause on the bra page in K-mart ads. But then I thought, what would Casanova do? Damn right he would follow her.

She drove an old blue-and-white Beetle with a university sticker on the back window. It figured. Ten minutes to a side street downtown. She hopped out and headed into the Brontosaurus, a hip-hop dance club. I'd never been in. Come to think of it I'd never been in any club. But a la Casanova: go where the women are. Or was that someone else?

The doorman or bouncer, bald and muscular, took my money. "Give me your hand."

"Why?" I asked.

"I have to mark you."

I gave him my hand and he drew a thick slash from my pinkie to the underside of my thumb.

The place reeked of beer, marijuana, and sweat–hope, desire, and piss. I felt vaguely like I was in high school again, which made me want to vomit. I saw Griffin moving from the bar with a green glass in her hand. To boost my courage, I thought of Casanova who by now would have romanced everyone in the place. I just had to do one.

I walked straight up to her. "Hey."

"Hello?" she asked.

"Remember me from the project?" She looked different, like she'd lost weight in her bones.

"No."

"Oh, I'm sorry." I couldn't even stalk the right woman.

"What's your name?" She put her thumb to her lips and chewed it with her canines.

"Lipton," I said.

"Lipton? Like the tea?"

"Yeah. It's the bane of my existence, the reason I can't be a movie star or a car salesman."

"You could change it."

"I can't think of anything better."

"Did you really think I was someone else?"

"Yeah."

"Oh." She took a sip from her green glass.

The rhythmic beat of dance mix was about to loosen my fillings and I was sure had already stripped all the screws in my glasses. Thinking the conversation over, I turned to leave. She grabbed my hand and put her drink in it. Then she produced a pen and replaced the drink with the pen.

"I have to find my friends, but write your number down, and I'll give you a call. I'll think of some name suggestions." She offered me her palm.

I wrote. And then I left. On the way back to my apartment, I remembered to ask for her number.

The next morning, I saw a beautiful, majestic white crane dead on the side of the road. How a crane got run over I didn't know. Maybe it didn't; maybe it had a heart attack in the air and just plopped down right there next to the road. Regardless, I had a dead crane on my hands. Bad omen. What was I to do with a dead crane? What would Casanova do?

After work, I went straight to Barnes & Noble and had five large coffees, one right after the other, as fast as I could. The caffeine pulsed through me, expanding the little veins in my head. My leg bounced of its own accord. By God, I'd have a woman, dead crane or no dead crane. Right after I went to the bathroom.

S. Craig Renfroe, Jr.

I started by cruising the university. The woman-who-was-not-Griffin might still be there. It was my experience that college was a place of dulled reflexes. Once entered, it seemed no one much had anywhere else to go. Everything was directed inward. And so I drove to the heart of the university but found only baseball-capped frat-boys and white t-shirted sorority sisters facing each other in rocking chairs with dueling speakers exchanging volleys of antagonistic tunes. Love was like that.

I gave up. Wasn't much of a try, but it was a big place and I was a small person. As I drove to the gate, I saw her smoking under a bus stop sign. I considered pulling up and giving her a ride but felt like one of those people who stop for hitchhikers. I pulled down into a neighboring lot. She didn't see me coming so I acted with pure Casanovian impulse and took her cigarette-free hand in both of mine.

Her startled look dragged words from me. "Ok, we don't really know each other, but I'm telling you fate wants us together and you know what they say about fate."

She yanked her hand away.

"We both happen to sign up for a stupid experiment and now we should get married. Is that it? What in the hell's wrong with you? You've been following me?"

Damn, I thought. Wrong one, again. That was the problem with griffins; they were shape-shifters, or was that chimeras?

"Help! Help!" She had a nice set of lungs despite the smoking. "Help!"

I ran. I wasn't convinced Casanova would have run. I rather thought he would've silenced her with a kiss, but then Casanova served time in prison, and I was willing to emulate him only so far.

Going up the sidewalk, I saw the lesbians reclined together on the foldout couch. One sat between the other's legs, and in the bluish glow of TV, the other one twirled strands of her lover's hair.

I got in and locked the door. The place smelled of convenience store cappuccino and old tuna. The answering machine light blinked red. I sat down and tried to turn on the TV with the remote. The batteries had died a week ago. I picked up the latest *Rolling Stone* and turned to the ads in the back. Under the picture of a bikini-clad woman was the number 1-900-HOT-FOXX. I dialed it.

"Hello, I'm Rachel and I've been waiting for you to call."

"Really?"

"Oh, yes. What's your name."

"Um. Cas."

"You have a very sexy voice, Cas."

"Thanks. You, too."

"You're really turning me on, Cas."

"I haven't done anything."

"What would you like to do?"

"I'm not sure. Should I ask what you're wearing?"

"A red teddy, but I could put on or take off anything you like."

"Don't go to any trouble."

"I like trouble."

"What do you look for in a man?"

"You."

"No, besides me. I mean generally what does a woman want."

"We want a man who cares about what we want, like you."

"Are you just saying that?"

"Oh no, that's an honest turn on. I'm very turned on."

"But I can't make it work. I don't know how to keep them interested. And then they move away or start screaming, and then what do I do? What am I supposed to do, Rachel?"

"You piss me off."

"Excuse me?"

"You piss me off," she said. "I come home today to find my damn water heater burst and my carpet soaked, an inch of water in the kitchen. The plumbers screw up the pipes so now I don't even have water. I've been up since six and you give me this bullshit. Look if you want to get off, get off. Otherwise, don't give me your crap."

"I think I'll just get . . . I mean hang up."

Rachel didn't say goodbye.

I could hear the shower start up next door. Sounded like he was alone. Casanova died at his friend's estate, alone, etching out his memoirs in his friend's library, reliving his escapades. I flipped through the *Rolling Stone* ads. A little one read, "Rocking Singles, matchmaker music style." I dialed. A machine told me to enter my zip-code.

"First entry," the machine voice continued. "Cynthia Shaw."

There was a click and a woman's voice: "This is Cyn. I'm into Joy Division, Misfits, anything off of Cleopatra records like Rosette Stone or Mephisto Walz."

The machine said, "Press one to leave a message for Cynthia Shaw."

I pressed one. "Hello, Cynthia. My name's Cas and I'm into the same kind of stuff. I really think Cleopatra rocks. I think we should get together. Maybe get a coffee at Barnes & Noble and we could swing by Century Music and check out the new releases. So, call me. . . . No. Forget that. Cyn, to tell you the truth, I made all that up. My name's not even Cas; it's Lipton. I don't like music unless it's on the soundtrack of a movie, and I don't know a damn thing about you, and I think this phone dating thing is a bunch of shit, and I think my grandfather might have died today, but I'm too much of a coward to check my messages even though that little red light is blinking away. I don't have any qualities to sell me. And I'm not going to make myself an ad. All I can say is I need someone, and you're the closest I got." I took a breath to rant some more, but the stupid machine cut me off.

"Thank you," it said. Then it demanded I type in my name and number.

I put the phone down and shook the remote control but the TV still refused to come on. So I rose out of my dying chair and went over to the answering machine. I hit the play button.

A woman's voice said, "How about Roland, Galahad, or Theseus?"

TICKLE, ME?

Paul got up from his mother's grave. Martha McClain Tickle, the stone said, in the line beside the other two: Patrick Stevens Tickle and Paul Tickle. Twenty years before, Paul's father, in a fit of morbidity, bought the plots and the head stones. Said if he were going to have to spend all that money anyway, he wanted his grave and tombstone while he could enjoy them. Paul moved over these two empty plots, walking over his own grave.

As he made his way to the town, the dawn broke, the sun flooding the place with the new day, beginnings. He watched the people scramble out of their homes and scurry to their cars as if the light were killing them.

His dad, still in his red robe, sat with remote control in hand, the colored light of the TV playing on his unshaven face.

"Dad?"

"Crazy for Coco Puffs?"

"You haven't got dressed yet."

"Just do it," his dad said.

"Yeah, just do it."

Paul took the remote and turned the set off. His dad looked up at him, his face blank like the screen.

"Go put on some clothes."

His dad got up.

"I have to go work." Paul raised his voice.

There was no reply from his dad's room. Paul laid the

remote on the arm of the recliner.

At work, Paul sat and watched. That was his job. Packer's Meat employed most of the town, people to process the animals into the packages where they stopped being animals and became food. Paul, after repeatedly vomiting on the evisceration line, had been reassigned to quality inspection. The company was allowed only so much "non-ingredient" content in their meats. They stationed him at the grinder vat, a huge hole; the "remains" of the meat that were dumped from a conveyer belt into the hole were ground into processed food. He had to watch and count the number of rats that fell into the vat. If too many fell in, he could push a button to stop the conveyer, and the vat was emptied. So he sat and watched.

Paul heard the woman come into the bar, the tap, tap of her high heels. She stood at the other end. She wore a coat quilted out of labels: Abercrombie & Fitch, Nike, Izod, Atlanta Braves, J-Sport, Duke; Tweety-Birds on both sleeves, Sylvesters on the elbows, an illegal Joe Camel patch on her breast, the South Park kids on the hem. He could hear her telling the bartender that she was going to make a hood out of some of her Starbucks shirts that were getting ratty.

The woman, complete with coat and drink, sat down next to him, crossing her legs toward him, one heel almost touching him. Paul watched his Guinness.

"So you don't like people?" she asked.

"No."

"How about me?"

"It's not that I don't like you in particular; it's just I don't like you in general."

She took a drink and ran her tongue around the lip of the cup. "I think you should like me."

"Why? What's so special about you?"

"I'm nice."

"There you go. I'm not nice."

"I heard you were a nice guy."

"Lies." Paul took a swig of his beer, nearly finishing it.

"I still think we should be friends."

"Ok, we're friends."

"I don't believe you."

"Then, what kind of friend are you?"

She stared at him, her eyes unblinking. She recrossed her legs, her knee to him. "I don't like you."

"See, I knew this was going to happen. I tried to warn you." Paul got up and walked out of the bar.

When he got home, he could hear his dad flipping through the channels. A Dentine commercial, flip, a sitcom canned laugh, flip, a Ford commercial, flip, a scream, flip, a wild animal sound, flip, a Coke commercial, flip. Paul went in and watched his dad, his endless quest through the channels for something that was never there.

"Dad, I'm going to fix beans and rice."

"What you talking about, Willis?"

"If you don't eat dinner, you don't get your Kit-Kat."

"Give me a break, give me a break, break me off a piece of that Kit-Kat bar."

"Go on and take your bath while I fix dinner."

His dad looked around, the space of the room

filled with the sound of a Head & Shoulders shampoo commercial. Paul went back to the kitchen.

The phone rang, rang. His dad flipped, flipped. Paul took the boiling rice off the burner and answered the phone. “Hello?”

“Are you Paul Tickle.”

“No.”

“I had a number that said for a good time call Paul Tickle.”

“Not him.”

“What should I do about my good time?”

“Find Paul Tickle.” Paul hung up.

He couldn’t sleep with the sounds of the house creaking into his half-waking dream. He put his robe on and went to the living room. His dad sat in front of the muted TV: flip, flip. Paul went to the kitchen and made himself some tea. There were lights on at the neighbors, and he could see a man and woman throwing their hands up at each other, their voices as mute as the TV. They had moved in when Ms. O’Connel had died. He watched them, each disappearing and reappearing in the window. The woman picked up an ash tray and threw it on the floor. The man looked out the window and saw Paul. As the man stared at Paul, the woman raged oblivious. Finally, the man walked over and pulled the blinds. The tea kettle blew.

When he left for work the next day, there was someone on the sidewalk, waiting. Paul walked past him. He could hear the man’s steps behind.

"Excuse me, sir."

Paul put his hands in his pockets.

"Sir?"

"Yeah," Paul said, still walking. He didn't look back.

"Are you Paul Tickle?"

"No."

"But, sir, I'm sure Mr. Tickle lives in that house you just left."

"I don't live there."

"Who does?"

"Paul Tickle." Paul heard the man slow his pace, the steps receding like a wave.

At Packer's, Paul saw the rats playing on the pipes, saw a big rat lose its footing and flip end-over-end to hit the lip of the vat and disappear inside. One. He made a note of it.

The woman with the label coat sat down next to him and motioned for the bartender. She took out a cigarette, a filter-less Camel. She smoked silently for a while. Paul drank faster, his glass half empty.

"So what's your name?" she asked.

The bartender, waving a rag around the bar as if he were cleaning it, looked up. "He's Paul Tickle."

"That's a funny name."

"You never heard of him."

"No, why?"

"He's famous."

Paul turned his drink up, but when he set it down, the woman pushed a full glass of Guinness over to him. Paul hesitated but then took up the new glass and swallowed.

The bartender continued, "There was this contest a few years ago. Four people had to live in this new Ford coupe and the one to stay the longest won the car. Well, Paul here he got chosen. They went in on a Friday and before the day was out this other wanker'd already given up. But not Tickle; no, he doesn't even get out of the car for the five minute breaks every two hours, except to go to the bathroom. He just sits there, in the passenger seat, staring off. Well, the town's all down there off and on and by Sunday another one's out. So it's down to Tickle and this girl. She switched seats every so often, but Paul just stayed on in the front passenger seat, wouldn't talk to no one, and stopped eating by Monday. They were in there for another three days till the girl said she had to go home to her baby and got out of the car."

The woman in the brand-name coat turned away from the bartender. "You stayed in a car for six days straight?"

Paul just drank.

"That's not all," the bartender said. "The officials declared him the winner, went over, opened the door, and handed him the keys to the new car. Well, Tickle takes a look at the keys and then the officials, closes the door and then locks them. Car had power locks, very nice. So Paul just sits there, like before."

"He'd already won."

"Yeah, he just sat there in the locked car. Half the town watched him, sitting, staring. After that if we saw somebody day-dreaming, we called it 'pulling a Tickle.'"

The woman was looking at Paul who was gulping his beer. "You're smirking."

Paul took his face out of his glass. "I hate that word, 'smirk.'"

"Well, you're smirking."

The bartender tapped the bar with a mug till the woman looked back over to him. "He wouldn't come out of that car. People kept asking him what he thought he was doing. Was it a political protest? Was he sick? Was he nuts? He ignored them all. The car lot owners weren't sure what to do–it was now legally his car after all. But it was on their property, so they got the police and a locksmith. When they got the door open, the police pulled him out. Tickle just walked away. Without a word."

The woman turned herself to face him; she reached out and caught his sleeve, the Nike swoosh touching him. "Why, Paul?"

He pulled away, downed the last of the beer, and left.

His dad was asleep in the recliner, Barbara Walters smiling at some smooth-faced actor. Paul left him there. He started cleaning, the kitchen, the bathroom, his room, his dad's. He worked well into the night, the odor of Lysol and Endust almost overpowering him. He finally stopped when he had worked his way back into the living room. The TV was off and his dad was watching him sweep the last bit of the hall.

"Kills germs," his dad said.

"Why don't you go to bed."

His dad held the remote control up in his hand like a wand. "When you care to send the very best."

"I love you, too."

His dad got up and wandered to his room.

S. Craig Renfroe, Jr.

His boss, wearing a tie pin with college fraternity letters, shook Paul's hand, the boss's hand palm down, the dominant animal. "We need to talk."

Paul nodded and turned back to the pipes and the rats' game of tag.

He ate his lunch there: three peanut butter sandwiches and a Mars bar. No one came up to the hole, except his boss to tell him he was doing a sorry job and that they would be installing motion sensors soon. His boss was new, had started a month ago, originally from Rome, Georgia. Paul chewed his Mars bar slowly, hoping it would last another ten minutes, when he would be allowed to start back to work.

With his day's watching over, he gathered his things and left before his boss could catch him.

As he walked down his street, Paul could see the white van, the one from the Home. The fighting neighbors were on the lawn, watching the hedges. And Paul could see the man from the other morning leading his dad down the steps. His dad still had the remote control in his hand.

Paul turned around and walked in the other direction.

The bar was festive, green and red Christmas lights everywhere; the new owners' idea, the bartender said, along with other changes, menus with a coat of arms, candles on all the tables, a CD changer playing New Age techno, drinks with straws with little hats. Paul stared into his Guinness's dark depths, a black hole.

The woman in the brand-name coat sat next to him. She was already smoking a filter-less Camel and let the smoke creep its way over to Paul. She ordered a drink with a funny straw.

"Paul," she said.

Paul ordered a double whiskey and took his beer and whiskey to a table by the window. He blew out the candle.

He had two more beers and another whiskey before the woman left. His glass almost empty, he swirled the black liquid, a twisting void. He heard a noise.

She'd knocked on the window and motioned for him to come outside; she was holding something. When he came out, she thrust her hands toward him. A small, brown-speckled bird peeked out between her fingers.

"Do you know anything about birds?" she asked.

"No."

"He was out by my car. Wouldn't move even when I walked up on him."

Paul shook his head and turned up his collar against the wind.

"What should we do with him?" she asked

"Is there an animal shelter about?" Paul asked.

"I don't know." She looked from the bird to Paul. Her eyes were wide with a kind of sympathy that Paul'd only seen on TV.

"He wouldn't move. I think something's wrong with him."

"Birds die." He didn't mean to say it. She didn't appear to notice.

"Are you okay?" she asked the bird. It turned its black eyes toward her. "What should we do?"

"I don't know."

She keep looking at the bird. "Paul?"

He didn't answer.

"Paul?"

He didn't answer.

"Paul, do something. Please."

Paul reached out, and she handed him the bird. He held it in his right hand and petted it. In one motion he twisted its head away from its body. There was a sound like a twig breaking.

"Oh my god. My god, my god, my god, my god, my god."

With the woman's prayer in the wind, Paul held the bird in front of him and walked away, down the street.

At the foot of his own grave, Paul kicked the ground with his boot heel. Getting on his knees, he found a rock and used it to scrape away at the shallow hole. He placed the bird there. He pushed the dirt back over the little corpse. The wind in the trees sounded like ghosts, ghosts who might not even have died yet but were waiting to quietly haunt those who would never hear them.

SUBMERSION

Howie and Alex know about the trespassing signs on the trees going up the drive, they've even been caught by Mr. Bumgardener before, but they still come through the woods so they can pretend they don't know, that they just happened on the pond. Howie follows his big brother up the bank and round toward the steep side. At first, riding their BMXs down the pond dam is thrill enough. But soon, they try tricks, popping wheelies on the way up, or jumping dirt clods and flying off humps. Howie wants Alex back up on the pond dam to watch a slanted jump from halfway down.

"You're a baby. Babies can't slant jump," Alex says.

Just as Alex reaches the top, two hands, enormous and stark white with yellowing cracked fingernails, reach out through the woody undergrowth surrounding the pond and push the tree limbs aside. A bulbous head, hairy and pudgy, pokes through, as large as one of the boys. Howie sees it above him. The head shaggy but clean, new.

"You're not real," Howie says.

The head looks down at Howie and then up to Alex, who's frozen, half out of his bicycle seat. One impossible finger points at Alex. "He exists, because he's there." The voice, high and childlike, surrounds them.

The thing emerges from the woods so huge its shoulders rise above the dam. Naked and splotchy, fat but square, it reminds Howie of a picture he'd drawn years ago when he'd finally stopped spinning the crayons in circles and tried to draw a person. Its breathing is slow and noisy, a bulldog's breathing. It shakes as if from a chill. Its eyes widen, the iris clear blue and large enough to count the pulsing blood vessels.

In two strides it stands between the brothers.

"Please don't eat us," Alex says.

"I get to meet her at last," it says.

Howie rides his bike up and behind the monster. He stops next to Alex, still frozen, still locked in fascinated fear.

"I will meet her," it says. And it steps into the pond, knee deep. It pauses, seems to breathe in the air, the moment. It continues, enough to cover its hairy lower back. Howie had daydreamed about how deep the pond went, where it went. The giant wades farther out, not stopping till it is submerged, till the water seals over the wound of its passing.

Howie nudges Alex to break his catatonic stare. Alex gets tripped up in his bike and falls to the ground. He jumps up as if the land were burning him. Howie peddles after Alex, away, as fast as they can, all tricks forgotten in trying to forget this last one.

Jill turns into the driveway, her headlights illuminating the familiar sign: "Bumgardener." It's been years since she's been here. She wouldn't be here now if she hadn't come for her dad–lot of good that did. He died before she made it down. Hours before. All that remained were the arrangements, and her mother and sisters could handle those.

The house looks the same. In the dark. In the day, her brother said it would look green instead of light yellow. She hopes not to stay long.

She goes to the door. Locked. When did they start locking it? She picks up the potted fern where their mother hid the key in a Ziploc bag for them after school, just in case. Only worms.

Someone would be home soon.

The moon, floodlight, casts everything in a daylight that isn't quite. Jill takes in the stars, stars she hasn't seen in as many years as the house, stars obscured outside her apartment by the perpetual city glow. She could take a walk in all this extraterrestrial light; she even casts a sickly shadow.

The walk from the patio leads through Mom's flower garden, herbs and shrubs farther on. As children, Jill and her siblings were charged with the upkeep of some of the path. She never enjoyed it, never came to accept the dirt on her hands, the sweat in her eyes. The path turns from smoothed stones to gravel, to packed dirt, the cultivation falling away as it progresses into the woods, into the true wild. She remembered the path as more civilized, but her parents had slowed down–her dad had stopped–and they had no more child labor. It goes on, the path, right down to the pond.

The garden was her mom's, but the pond was Dad's. There'd been a spring, and though he'd hired a bulldozer to deepen it, much of the pond was hand dug. Dad spent his afternoons and weekends with a shovel and a pickax. Piles of dirt. Clods. Buckets and wheelbarrows. Tireless hours, in drought and shower, in sopping mud and ice-clumped soil. Unlike the garden, the kids were never forced to help, in fact, were never invited. Her brother shoveled sometimes, but in silence, unthanked. Dad would talk with Jill on the sidelines, but only in monosyllabic reply to whatever direct question she put to him. No one in the family seemed to understand, Jill least of all. What was he digging for?

The night is warm and humid. The water doesn't move, is still, expectant.

To her, the pond was a hole, a pockmark on the earth, where Dad would rather spend his time than with his kids–not would, had. She'd never fished, like her sister. And the one time she went swimming here, in the brown depths, she'd gotten an ear infection. But now, she has a hard time pulling up the old resentment toward this moonlight-painted place. Across from her, a pine hangs off the shore, leaning out over the water, as if it's looking at its reflection.

Would there be digging in heaven?

How long has she been crying? She steps into the shallow end graded for minnow beds, the water cool, a little shocking. She steps down with her other foot, committed. In. She wades on, the muck sucking at her shoes. The mud claims one. With each inch of her calves covered by the pond, she shivers, but feeling the cold water, the primitive circuit of nerves-impulse-brain, keeps her from thinking about anything. Over her knees, it soaks the hem of her skirt, weighing it down. Then the cotton floats indecently with air trapped beneath. Bubbles. The wet, solid air rises around her legs, creeping up. Her next step doesn't touch bottom, her other foot sliding. She's under, below, the rest of her embraced by the cold and the pressure at once. What if she doesn't come back up, what if she doesn't bother, what if she goes instead down farther to wherever this goes? She comes out cracking the air with slaps on the surface. She spits and kicks. She could drown alone out here. In this place her father made.

Instead, she lets the water hold her, lift her up.

S. Craig Renfroe, Jr.

PAST THAT

Samantha, who I hadn't seen since she left me to marry her fiancé seven years ago, sat at the Waffle House booth with Desmond across from her. I had loved her but could never tell her so and, despite making love to as many women that would allow me, had yet to love any one of them the same. During college, Sam–she went by Sam then–Desmond, and I had all spent countless hours in there, drinking coffee till our hands shook. Now, Sam was back but only for the Lossdor University Arts Festival. She was an artist. I'd been an artist, too, but I hadn't made it. She made mosaic pottery out of broken pots, creating new out of old–I couldn't help wondering what she would make from our past over the next two days. What would I do?

Sam was talking to Liddy, a waitress she'd lived with. Hit by the rising cost of Lossdor U., she'd moved in with Liddy and actually waitressed at the Waffle House from time to time. I hadn't gotten to know Liddy–it'd never occurred to me.

When I sat down beside Desmond, Sam said, "Did you know Liddy is dead?"

"She looks fine to me." Though in truth, she didn't. Cigarette in one hand, coffee cup in the other, she stood beside the table, barely able to keep her shoulders up, as though the weight of the air could topple her at any second, the weight of all the poverty and desperation and grease that had so attracted me to this place.

"First thing I hear when I get back is that Liddy's

dead," Sam said. "I'm staying at the Valley Inn, and I asked the Greek girl at the counter if she knew if Liddy still worked there on the weekends. And the girl said, 'No, she's dead.' That's the way she said it: 'No, she's dead.' I was horrified. I'm not back five minutes, and already I find out one of my friends is dead. So I call Desmond to tell him to come right over, and we came straight here. Who's working, but the dead woman herself."

Liddy looked away through most of this and by the end sat down next to Sam, as if the weight were finally too much for her.

"How are you?" Sam asked me, as if I'd come here straight from my Aesthetics class ready to bitch, as if this weren't the first time we'd seen each other in seven years. For an instant, I wished that Greek girl from the motel had told her I was dead.

"Fine," I said.

"I like the hair, Louis."

I had grown my hair out long, a subtle, most likely futile, protest to my job teaching art in middle schools–multiple schools because the educational cuts on the arts made a full-time position at any one school impossible. Sam had cut her beautiful hair off, a few spiky unkempt sprigs sticking out an inch or two, like a tropical rainforest ravaged by clear cutters.

"Thanks," I said.

"Desmond tells me you buy fancy shampoos and conditioners for your hair."

"Does he?" I ask.

Desmond didn't add anything, though I glanced over at him.

"Someone taught me to use conditioner."

I tried to intrigue her with that "someone," but she didn't seem to hear me, her eyes focused off somewhere else, somewhere internal, the way she used to, her green eyes so clear and luminescent I could hardly bear them. This isn't how it goes, I thought; this isn't how I imagined her coming back to me.

She turned to Liddy and rattled off questions about old friends. Desmond and I fell into idle chat. Unlike Sam who after graduation abruptly disappeared from our lives, we saw each other once a week. We talked on occasion about Sam, always in terms alive with the recollection of her, and perhaps we only continued to be friends in order to prolong that shared dream. Desmond had known her longer; they'd been two years ahead of me. He introduced us. It was their last semester at Lossdor. And I knew that she was engaged, so before I even saw her, I promised myself I wouldn't waste my time. Shortly thereafter, I, of course, fell madly in love with her.

"You're a little sunburnt," Desmond said.

"My brother bought a kayak," I said. "So we took it up to the lake."

Sam and I used to create a rhythmic day, meeting after each class at the Waffle House or Liddy's house, staying up till three in the morning, then sleeping and going to classes, and doing it all again. We would sit on Liddy's porch, and I would snap twigs while Sam told me about the drug dealer she'd dated and how she didn't like sex and her desire never to have children. None of that mattered to me. I could give up sex–or I could at least please myself. And who wanted kids? I just wanted her. She never spoke of her fiancé, except once to say she couldn't wait to take his last name (Hartis) so she could be rid of her own (Bumgardner). I thought at the time that was the reason she was marrying him, and my name (Garrow) was at least as pleasing if not more. I was stupid enough to think we were courting, that I was stealing her away.

The night before her graduation, we stayed out till five in the morning, and as I followed her back toward Lossdor, she threw a lit cigarette out her window, and in the dark it exploded on the road in a fiery red tornado. And it was gone. After the ceremony, after I gave her a piece of pottery I'd made, after she introduced me to her parents, her sister, and her fiancé, she was gone.

I found myself in the mall, calling all the friends I knew to see if they wanted to watch a movie or play pool, anything, but they weren't there. I stood in the mall, with people conspicuously consuming all around me, and none of them would remember that precise moment, remember that I was standing at the phone booth or even if they did, would have no idea that was the moment I realized she was gone. In order not to break down in front of the Foot Locker, I convinced myself I could relive those months over in my mind, I could draw strength from knowing I'd experienced a masterpiece, as if I'd dated Rossetti's *Elizabeth Siddal*.

But Desmond would ruin that.

He controlled everything around him, everything about him an act of will, even something as spontaneous as laughing. He refused to laugh, refused to surrender to laughter, an involuntary act, an acknowledgment of something outside himself. Desmond would have nothing to do with it. As we watched movies, he would sit silently as the rest of us howled. But he did laugh–on his own terms. He would choose the most inappropriate moment and come out with this obviously forced guffaw, loud and protracted. Who would notice the person laughing with the rest? Who wouldn't notice the laugh out of place? He was perhaps my best friend.

Sam went on chatting with Liddy–what was she to Sam? What was I?

Another Waffle House waitress refilled my coffee cup faster than I could drink it. I have a compulsion where I must finish anything set before me. I keep drinking though I'm not thirsty–under the influence of diligent servers, I've made myself sick.

Desmond and I were sitting in silence. I was waiting for him to say something about me kayaking.

"Kayaking reminds me of the novel I'm writing," Desmond said. "Not that there's a kayak in it. It's about NASCAR."

Desmond was a writer, and that was how he ruined my past. He published a story about Sam and himself, though he called it fiction and changed the names (Joey and Damon). In the story ("Almost Home"), he made out like he and Sam would have been together if not for a comedy-of-errors involving their first date. He took plenty of poetic license in making Sam adore him, loving his great mind and his verbal wit–despite the fact that Sam had told me many times she found him full of shit. The final scene took place as Sam was about to leave Lossdor because of her financial troubles and Desmond showed up to help her pack. Before they knew it, Sam took off her tattered sweatshirt with thumb holes in the sleeves, and they were embracing. I could barely finish reading. This was a woman who didn't like sex? To his wife Patricia, who did like sex, Desmond pointed out he was a fiction writer and "Joey" had no relation to Sam at all, except in some incidentals–the raw stuff of story-making. To me, he said no such thing. Even though the story occurred before I knew either one of them, I felt like Desmond had co-opted my memories, that he'd sullied them, stolen from them. My Sam would never act that way, my Sam would never think that way, my Sam would never press her teeth into his shoulder that way. But hadn't it been Desmond who Sam contacted first? Hadn't she sought him out through the Internet? Hadn't he been the one she called when she got back?

Just as I'd begun to worry if Sam was ever going to talk to us, Liddy got up from the table to go work. Then Sam talked. In fact, she wouldn't shut up. She told us how she was addicted to caffeine, how she drank three pots of coffee a day, how she quit smoking, how she painted on the roof, how she became obsessed easily, how she feared being bitten on the toe by a rabid bat as she slept, how she gave up coffee, how she took up jogging, how she became obsessed with jogging, how she jogged miles to the grocery store and jogged back with a backpack filled with canned foods she didn't need, how she lost sixty pounds, how she woke up one day and quit jogging completely, how she continued to take a blind coworker to work though she'd quit after she started making enough money off her pottery, how she wished she could run an antique store, how she read five books a week. I listened–betrayed by so much–and drank my bottomless cup of coffee.

S. Craig Renfroe, Jr.

Finally, Desmond said, “We should head toward Lossdor.”

We were going to see Doc Watson, one of the headliners at the festival. Desmond offered to drive us all (Control! Control!).

Sam turned to me in the backseat. “Do you remember the time you told me some woman spat at me?”

“No.” I didn’t.

“We were leaving the Waffle, and I was driving. You said that a woman walking across the parking lot spat at my car. That’s the word you used, ‘spat.’ I’d never heard anyone use that word. And I keep wondering what it was I did to make that woman so angry. What could I have done to make someone spit at me.”

“I don’t remember it.”

“That’s one of the few clear memories of back then. I think I have early Alzheimer’s. I remember that about you. About Desmond, I mainly remember when he told Patricia to put down a cookie because it would go straight to her hips.”

Desmond said, “They do. She told me to get on her about that.”

“That’s all you remember?” I asked.

“Yeah. I can read a novel and then start again at page one because I’ve already forgotten it.”

“So do you read the same five books every week?” I asked.

A witness to a woman who spat at her? That was how she remembered me; that was all I occupied in her memory when I had given her so much room in mine?

The auditorium of the new Fine Arts Building was full, and we were an hour early. We still managed to get seats very close to the front, though we were sandwiched in by the elderly. I sat through Sam's dissertation on why her sister married the wrong man, but when she started cataloguing all the changes to Lossdor, changes Desmond and I knew already, living here, I had to get away. It took me several minutes to excuse myself through the chiffon and slacks of our neighbors and head for the lobby.

I got over her. I got over Sam. I tried not to compare other women to her or hold her up as some kind of mental standard. I could find enough problems with them without her help. But in the back of my mind I did think about her, I did fantasize about when we would meet again later in life. No, not fantasize. There was never any images, never any story lines; it was just a feeling, an indomitable expectation that we would come together again. And so we had.

Outside the auditorium, Dr. Sommers stopped me with a gentle hand. "Louis, how have you been?" She was still as beautiful as when she'd taught us Painting and Art History, but I could see the lines breaking from the corners of her eyes and the cords in her neck slightly protruding. Desmond, an Art minor, once said she'd asked him to dance at a party when she was drunk. She'd once told me that my brush strokes were not bad, just overstated.

"I'm happy to be back," I said.

"We're so glad you alumni came for this. What are you doing now?"

"Teaching."

She brushed her lips with her thumb. "Where?"

"Middle schools."

"Oh." She lowered her thumb. "You're fighting the good fight. Have you seen *Pollack*?"

"No."

"It's very good. Weren't you the one who liked Pollack?"

"No."

"Maybe that was your friend Sam."

"She's here."

"Oh, I'll have to see her."

"She's down toward the front."

"Looks crowded. I'm sure I'll see her at her pottery exhibit tomorrow. You'll be there won't you?"

"I don't know."

"Good. I'll see you there." She floated off.

I looked at the CDs for sale, some of the paintings and sculpture, also for sale. I talked to people I vaguely knew who vaguely knew me in terms even vaguer. The lights lowered, and I followed the stragglers reluctantly in. Getting back into my row created a ruckus because the elders were too fragile to withstand my passing, so the whole row up to Sam had to clear out to let me in.

As soon as I took my seat, I realized I had to pee. Not that nagging premonition where there was something that needed doing, like the returning of overdue videos. Not that firm feeling, like you needed to eat or you could use a drink when you stopped to get gas. Not even a direct necessity, like wanting to move your leg that had fallen asleep. This was the alarm clock across the room playing at full volume Beethoven's Fifth while the intermediate beeps drove the neighbor's dog to howling. This was unbearable, and Doc Watson hadn't set foot on the stage. How many cups of coffee had I had? I took a deep breath. Calm, I thought, calm. I spelled the word out for myself and saw it in big letters slowly scrolling through my mind's eye. There. It'd passed, and now I could concentrate on the blind musician being led out on stage. I could think about his life. I could really go to the bathroom. Doc Watson made some jokes and talked a while about his informal appearance–another joke–and the songs he would play us. I turned to Sam. She was whispering to Desmond. What were they saying? I tried to get angry at their conspiracy, but all I could feel was the pressure building in my kidneys. Or was that the bladder? Calm, I thought, calm. Doc was into another song. I'd never known before how much the base of a guitar resembled a bedpan. I considered getting up. What would Doc Watson care? But as I looked down the line of old people in my way, their legs luxuriously extended, a few crossed at the ankles, they might as well have been Checkpoint Charlie. Clam, I thought, clam? I could see a clam in some comedy routine shooting out a stream of chowder at some unsuspecting boob. That beautiful stream. This couldn't be healthy. At least for the first time that night, I was unconcerned and unaware of Sam. I found myself on a sea, riding the swells and lulls. At moments the wave would crest, and I'd be certain any second I would wet my pants. And then it would subside again, though I could continually feel the presence, the eye of the hurricane. Doc strummed out more folksy blues gospel I was sure I'd have loved, had the flood waters not been rising. My kidneys and bladder both were about to rupture.

It would be blood, piss, and bile. Fuck this, I thought, prepared to blitz the old folks. But Doc said he would play three more songs before the intermission. Intermission! I'd waited this long; I'd be a damned fool not to wait it out.

Doc finished that third song, and I was out of my seat still clapping. Some of the elders made to get up, but I leapt over them like they were subway turnstiles. I headed for the bathroom. To Sam, Desmond once described the male orgasm as the feeling of urinating after holding it in for a very long time. I looked forward to the greatest orgasm of my life.

The white of the restroom blinded me. The walls were white. The floor tiles were white. The sink and countertop were white. The ceiling was white. The flourescent lights were white. The urinals were white. The reflection in the mirror was white. It was heaven's antechamber. I moved slowly toward the white. Slowly because even though I'd run, others in the back had already formed a line, and as I waited, a crowd, a mob, formed behind me, stretching out the door and into the lobby, with the pressure in their bowels manifested in their shuffling, coughing presence.

To my chagrin, I saw there was only one toilet and two low set urinals. Worse, there was no divider between the two urinals. I prayed for the sanctuary of the toilet. My turn came, and a spindly-legged teen flushed and moved off to the sink to zip, leaving me with the unavoidable open spot at the urinal in the middle of the toilet wall and the other porcelain trough. I took my place. With hands fanned, I fumbled my penis out.

I awaited the blissful floodgate release. I could feel it rising, rising, and it stopped. I'd frozen up. I was petrified. I could no more pee than I could afford not to pee.

Nothing. I'd never had this problem–this was the field of standup comics, kidney stoners, and homophobes. The person beside me flushed and was replaced immediately. I waited. Another took his place at that urinal. Out of the corner of my eye, I could see the strong, steady stream, mocking me. I had to do something; people knew me here. I stared at the urinal with its blue mat thingy and its urinal cake and its brand-name Toto label. Toto. Who the hell needs to be reminded of the dog from *The Wizard of Oz* when they go to the bathroom? What does Oz have to do with pissing? I'm on my way to see the wizard because I need to find a way to relieve myself. The more I tried the more it receded. I clenched, flexed, and extended muscles I didn't know existed. Anything that would move down there, I moved. The ones waiting surely must of known what had happened. They were making odds as to how long I'd continue to stand there, keeping up the charade. I waited out three more neighbors. It wouldn't come, and I felt sick from trying to force it. I would've settled for vomiting just to put something in that damn bowl, but even that failed me. I flushed, futilely.

As I washed my hands in shame, sure everyone was laughing at my play act to save face, someone slapped me on the back. Tadlock. We'd graduated together. He'd made erotic sculpture that had won him gallery space, prizes, and sex with several coed artists though he'd been married even then. He'd unsuccessfully tried to seduce Sam. At the time, I thought it my triumph he never succeeded.

"What are you doing?" he asked.

"Teaching middle school. You?"

"I'm in concrete."

"You work with concrete?"

"I pour it. Slabs."

We were silent, both in awe of how easily our lives could be summed up.

Back with Sam and Desmond, I said, "I saw Tadlock."

"Who?" she asked.

My memories kept depreciating. Doc Watson took the stage, and I didn't have to answer.

I sat through the rest of the concert with the need to pee fading, but with its passing, the pressure and urge to understand Sam rose, and even more pressing was the urge to reclaim her. She didn't look my way or nudge me. Through all the lyceums we'd been required to attend at Lossdor, she'd given me her snide asides–the smell of Pantene in her hair intoxicating me. And now we watched Doc Watson, and all I wanted was to leave.

When it had ended, we were all on our feet clapping, except Desmond who sat with his arms folded (Look at me! Look at me!).

"You want to hang out?" Desmond asked with no implication one way or the other that I could tell.

"I don't know." I tried to think of an excuse, but they knew I'd already taken off work to go to tomorrow's exhibits. Any excuse would be a clear lie. "I don't know."

"We're going to get beer and go back to Sam's fancy motel room."

"Sure," I said.

"You ever been kayaking, Sam?" Desmond asked.

"Is this something you've done or Louis?"

"Louis."

There was the miscarriage of a pregnant pause.

"I can't believe how things have changed," Sam said. "Lossdor didn't even have a gas station, and now it's got three fast food restaurants. That's progress."

She had repressed my past, and now she was ignoring my present. As we rode to the BiLo below the Valley Inn, I aimlessly plucked the strings from my black sweater that had the nasty habit of fraying.

In the store, Sam grabbed a bag of salted peanuts as we wandered toward the beer. They talked Milwaukee's Best and Rolling Rock, New Castle today and the yesterdays of Southpaw.

"Louis doesn't drink beer," Desmond said.

"Oh?"

"He prefers vodka."

"Really?"

"Yes," I said. I'd given it up because of the danger involved. I'd once, when safely drunk, cuddled with a woman who'd spent the next month convinced we were in love.

"Foster's!" Sam laughed.

Desmond guffawed. "I can't believe you drank so many that night."

Sam finally talked straight to me. "The first time I went over to Desmond's dorm room, we had Foster's, and I downed two of them right away."

"Really," I said.

"You read about it, Louis," Desmond said. "It happened just the way I wrote it."

Sam didn't seem to hear. Had she read Desmond's

story? Was her silence admission? Was it ignorance or indifference? Was it shame at not having read it? Maybe all Desmond's memories were true. Maybe they had slept together. Why did their possible, seven-year-old lovemaking bother me so much in the refrigerated beer section of a grocery store? They got a six pack of Foster's.

Her motel room matched perfectly the exterior of Valley Inn, dilapidated, tarnished, depressing. I'd never dared visit Sam when she and Liddy worked nights in the lobby. She showed us around, noting the torn lamp shade, the graffiti on the baseboard, the dresser missing a drawer–"Who would steal one drawer?" We started drinking, a beer apiece. I finished first. I needed it, but also it gave me something to do instead of just listening to Sam and Desmond roll around in nostalgia, like pigs in a sty, rutting in their past. I got another one, and Desmond went to the bathroom.

"You should have Desmond tell you about his grandfather setting a mule's tail on fire and letting it loose in a general store."

I had heard that story. I had heard it enough times to repeat it word for word. I had even read its unpublished written form. He had told that story at least once every two weeks at the Waffle. *That* she remembered. I should have repeated my love for her over and over. I should have chanted it in class, in her car, on Liddy's porch. I should have written it in papers, embroidered it on shirts, tattooed it on my face. She should remember it, goddamn it.

Desmond came back.

"Tell Louis about your grandfather and the mule."

I took the first gulp of my new beer, and the pressure was back, all of it, all at once, as if that last bit were all I could hold. Without a word, I headed for the bathroom, spared temporarily that poor mule.

I could say that she started it by treating me badly, by refusing to remember our past the way I did. I could say it was the beer. But, in truth, there's never a real good reason to explain why you've acted like an ass. I peed on the bathtub handles, both hot and cold, and the spout. I peed on the drain and the tacky traction flowers they'd put down. I even managed to pee on the soap holder. And still I was going strong. I made a line over the toilet, a quick circle around the seat, a light jump up to the handle. Over to the counter, I hit the unwrapped hotel soap and over the knobs for the sink. I finished on the hand towel.

They weren't talking when I came out. Both staring at the TV, Kevin Costner dancing with some wolves. I hated Kevin Costner.

"You need to go?" Desmond asked.

"Yeah." Though, I should have said, not anymore.

We took Sam's new Ford Explorer. When we got to the Waffle House, she stopped and I hopped out.

"See you tomorrow," Sam said.

"Sure."

Sam and Desmond drove off into the night together. To do what, I didn't know.

Those who believe in doing good fail to recognize the most underrated of human motives: spite. There is a cold joy in deliberately choosing to do wrong. I was well aware that I should've put my apparently fantasized relationship with Sam to rest, that I should've embraced the real person before me, that I should've developed some kind of healthy friendship with her where I supported her independent decisions while opening myself up to be vulnerable to her emotional needs, sharing with her so that she could realize my own needs. But, instead, during the drive home, I was happily thinking about how I'd pissed all over her bathroom.

I slept the pleasant sleep of the spiteful.

Like a second date, I fidgeted with my hair in the rearview mirror, nervous as to how she would react to my actions the night before. Nervous, but unrepentant. In fact, I couldn't wait to see her reaction, and I played different scenarios over in my head, each more dramatic than the next. The one I had going when I reached the Fine Arts Center featured her silently slapping me.

The sign outside of the room read "Repottery: Revealings. A showing of ceramic art by Samantha Hartis."

Pots in display cases lined the walls, and larger ones sat on angled tables in the center of the room. Sam stood by the tables talking with Dr. Sommers. I circled the room as briskly as I could, in case Sam chose to ignore me. Moving closer to the center, I felt like she wouldn't even acknowledge my presence, a final repudiation. Turning to the tables, I caught sight of a blue fragment in the mosaic covering an urn. The blue surrounded the raised line of a black S. That was mine. I'd given her a pot I'd made for a graduation present. I wasn't a thrower, but Sam'd spent some time getting me interested and teaching me, so I secretly worked on a present before she left. I decorated it with an "S" pattern and glazed it a sky blue–her favorite color. She'd told me no one had ever made her anything, and she'd hugged me for a long time, time enough to make me nervous as her family and fiancé watched on. Had she broken it during a move? Had she broken it on purpose? Did she even remember who'd made it?

"Why didn't you tell me?" she asked, angrily.

"What?"

"What?" She shook her head. "Desmond told me."

"He did?"

"You should have told me you were sick."

"Sick?"

"You don't have to put up a front. You're a real trooper for taking that shit last night and not feeling well."

Even my spite had been stolen from me.

"I want to buy one of your works. That one." I pointed to the urn that had digested my pot. I thought that might spark something in her. It didn't.

"I'll put you down, and they'll mail it to you after the show."

"No, I want it now."

She heard it in my voice. I hoped she heard it all.

She made arrangements and brought over a box.

"I'll carry it out. I don't need a box."

She startled me by taking my hand. "I was so happy to see you. I'll try to come down again. Before seven years this time."

I managed, "Good to see you, too."

She let my hand go, and I took her urn.

Outside, in the parking lot next to her Explorer, I held the urn tight, ready to dash it to pieces on the asphalt by her door. The weight of its creation held me at bay. I knew at least about making something, taking the raw and molding and combining and shaping, to bring order and form to incite beauty and joy. The reds of what looked like earthy brick that she'd placed at the apex of each of my fragments highlighted the sky blue, brought it to life in my hands. The "S" shapes contoured to the neck of the urn and led the eye down its length. The irregularities were like so many fortunate accidents, the little mishaps that made a trip memorable.

I set it gently in my passenger seat and closed the door. I opened the door again and put the seatbelt around it. Around the pieces of me in the design of her. We were together. We would always be together.

AN URBANE COMEDY
In Four Parts

Part I: A Nude Introduction

What if you woke up one morning in a musical? Kind of like the guy/roach in that Kafka story. But you're not a roach. You're fine. It's everybody else who's screwed up. They just start singing for no apparent reason, and when they're finished, they go on about their business as if nothing happened. Could you act like everything was normal while a tenor sings you rhyming directions to the closest Wal-Mart? Could you adapt? Would you start singing in the rain and in the subway? How could you tell if the whole world had gone mad or just you?

See that's my problem. Not that one day I woke up in a musical. I wish my waiter would burst into song detailing the Seven Courses of Denny's.

But no, I woke one day to find that every single woman in the world, or at least every single one I could lay my eyes on, had become a nudist. Not one woman wore a single stitch of clothing. Not the morning news anchor. Not my mother. Not my sister. Not the pedestrians. Not the students. Not my professor. Not one female. They were all inexplicably naked. At first I was horribly embarrassed for them and me.

"What's wrong? Is something wrong with me? Do I have a booger hanging out my nose?" my sister had asked.

"No," I'd murmured and ran out the door, hoping the

women getting a college education would be immune to the Empress's New Clothes syndrome.

The coeds were on the naked bandwagon as well, but I must admit I wasn't terribly disappointed. Particularly when I discovered they weren't averse to prolonged looks. It was amazing how many times Cynthia Long–a picture of magazine beauty–was going my way. Or I hers.

My face blushed perpetually; my eyes wondered wildly. A week passed. No one put on any clothes. And worse yet, no one seemed to notice. But I noticed and noticed and noticed. Hag and child, model and waitress, black and white. They were all equal in my naked eye. I was actually getting used to it. Or rather, used to enjoying it. For awhile, constantly seeing women in the buff had a tendency to excite me, but very soon it become more frustrating than enjoyable. Soon after that, it became damn irritating. I needed some explanations.

"What are you wearing?" I asked the girl closest to me in English class.

"It's a Hard Rock Cafe t-shirt. Can't you read?"

Obviously, she was mentally disturbed.

"What color is your shirt?" I asked a woman in the hall.

"Blue. Why? You color blind?"

Interesting.

"What kind of fabric is that?" I asked a female sitting at the cafeteria table near me.

"Cotton, I guess. Why?"

A pattern was forming.

"That's a nice shirt," I said to the check-out girl in the grocery store.

"Thanks."

More proof.

"I like those jeans," I said to a girl in the mall.

"I'm wearing a skirt, freak."

Well, there you go. I had come to the firm conclusion that the female populace was laboring under the false assumption that they were still dressed. So we come back to my earlier point: had all the women of the world gone mad or was I just bonked on a rush of bad hormones? Either way, I wanted the naked women out of my head.

I needed to try some experiments. I had to have irrefutable proof that these people were not pulling one over on me. So I flipped on *Baywatch*. I had heard TV can warp your view of reality, but I was hoping it would support mine. The shows must have been taped before all this, so the women should, in theory, be suitably clothed, or at least as suitably clothed as the women get on that particular show. They were not, however. After the show went off, I puzzled over the new information.

My dilemma came down to three possibilities. (1) Through some freak of nature or man, I had acquired a uniquely useless but extremely entertaining X-ray vision. (2) I had gone stark-raving mad. (3) I had encountered something supernatural which, by definition, defied explanation.

The solutions to my problem depended on these possibilities. If one was the case, then I'd have to submit to scientific analysis. Since I did not savor the idea of dissection or whatever the sanitized torturers of medicine and science might do, I disregarded this option. If two was the case, then I could find help in the area of psychology or psychiatry. But the psychologists would want me to spend years in couch talk with minimal results and maximum bills, and the neuro-scientists would give me a steady diet of pills with side-show side-effects. I didn't have the time and money for good ole psychology, and I didn't have the stomach for the brave new branch. Finally, I decided three must be the case, and so God help me.

Part II: The Devil Doesn't Like Dresses

I haven't gone to church with any regularity for over ten years. The little gravel parking lot and the scraggly lawn where people really parked are paved now. The four-room, free-standing building where Sunday school was held has been absorbed into the brick complex growing out of the rear of the church. It's still called "First Hope Baptist," but the weather-stained pine sign has been replaced by one of those tacky plastic gas-station ones where you can put the letters in rows to spell out prices or, in this case, messages like the one today: "God understands." Thank God, He does, since I surely don't.

I hope I'm not too underdressed in my blue t-shirt and jeans. My chuckle brings some rough stares from the people gathered in the antechamber waiting to get into the chapel. For the most part, they're suited men with somber faces and naked women with elaborate methods for keeping their hair suspended in the air. Some dressed-down young guys mull around in the back, so I work my way over to them keeping my eyes averted from the cellulite. Several girls are in the group. We exchange pleasantries, and I move off a comfortable distance as they resume their community gossip.

An auburn-haired girl in her early twenties walks toward me. She's tall, spindly, and small breasted. Her skin's an indoor pale; her shoulder-length hair's wiry and uncontrollable. She's definitely not Cynthia Long.

"You look nervous," she says.

"Yeah, I guess I am."

"First time in a church?"

"No, I used to go to this one as a matter of fact. But that was about ten years ago."

"Really? I've been going here all my life, and I don't remember you."

"We only came on holidays. You know, Christmas and Easter. That sort of thing." I scratch the stubble on my chin; I've been too distracted to shave lately. I try to keep my eyes on a print of Noah's arc being trashed on a darkened sea. Am I behaving like this because she's unattractive or because I respect her? I ponder this a few seconds before realizing that leaning against the wall beside the picture is a blonde with perfectly round breasts that stand four inches from her chest.

"Why'd you sigh like that?" The plain girl catches me off-guard, so I look at her but register only the almost invisible hairs around her belly button.

"Uh, no reason," I say. What's with the interrogation? She couldn't know. Could she?

Most of the others have filed in, so she turns to follow. For all her other shortcomings, she does have a nice rear. I probably shouldn't be thinking these things in church. I'm here to get help, and I'm already pissing God off. The young people sit toward the back, but since the chapel's not full, there are five empty pews left behind them. The plain girl with a nice butt follows her friends into the sixth pew from the back. I stop at the fourth. She looks back at me disapprovingly but faces forward when the music stops and everyone sits down.

So now what? How do I get God's attention? They're all praying now, but I doubt the deacon's going to mention my particular problem. I guess I could send up a personal prayer, but how do you word something like this? "Dear God, put some clothes on these silly women. Amen." Yeah, that'll work. How about: "God, stop giving me my own private Playboy vision. Hallelujah." Maybe if I get a little more sacrilegious a bolt of lightning will put me out of my misery. Although, if that blonde keeps turning this way, I wouldn't be that miserable.

Here comes the choir. What poor taste. The men come marching in wearing new-looking blue robes, and the women come in the buff. The preacher informs us that the gasoline tanker leading the choir is Mrs. Henderson. She takes a seat right in my line of sight. I can't keep from looking at her, like a moth to a welder's torch. Those mammoth thighs are road-mapped with blue veins trekking up varicose rises to look over scenic pock parks. I'm going to be sick.

I keep my eyes closed for most of the sermon, occasionally nodding off and jumping awake only to find myself staring straight into the thighs of death. Like most preachers, Rev. Johnston emphasizes the wrong syllables and speaks with increasing volume as he goes along; must be some kind of job-specific speech impediment. The only thing I like about the man is the content of his sermon. He talks about how easy it is to destroy something, but it's hard to create something, and so we should respect and love God's creations. Of course, the sermon's too long since I can sum it up in one sentence, except for all those Bible verses. I guess I like it because it reminds me of that comedy by Dante. Dante's lost in the woods and all, but because he loves this chick Beatrice, she gets him out, and he even gets to see God. Come to think of it, Dante was too long too.

The sermon's over and three-fourths of the congregation is still naked. Maybe the scientists will be gentle.

Rev. Johnston finishes and then after a meaningful-meaningless silence says, "And don't forget to come to our night meeting on the Devil's active role in the world. Deacon James, will you lead us in the closing prayer?"

The devil? The Devil. The Devil! Why didn't I think of that? It's so damn obvious. I mean, who else would do this sort of thing? He's trying to steal my soul with lust, and he's tormenting me at the same time. Tricky devil.

Then again, what if God's put this curse on me, like putting Dante in the woods, so I can learn to appreciate His creation and from there learn to love Him? Maybe all the women in the world are my Beatrice. But one more look at Mrs. Henderson's thighs convinces me: it has to be the work of the Devil.

Part III: Hell, Or a Hot Date

With several hours to spare before I see if Rev. Johnston knows how to fight the Devil, I visit Sade, the only person I have kept in touch with since the haze of high school. The smoke cloud greets me at the door; a combination of cinnamon incense and clove cigarettes can't disguise the heavy marijuana. I push on through the gas chamber, arriving at a clearing with a rickety fan, a flowery recliner, and a maroon couch. The fan churns out chilled air-conditioned air, making the room unnaturally cool. In the chair sipping a glass filled with a water-like substance is Sade. Unconscious on the couch is his younger sister, Laura. She's incredibly thin and doll-like. In fact, that's what she is: a black-haired, drugged-out, anatomically correct Barbie sprawling on a dingy, ripped couch. I keep my eyes on Sade, mostly.

"Hey, it's Richie Rich!" He knows I hate that.

"You know I hate that, Sad Sack." He winces satisfactorily. "Why's Laura here?" I ask.

He looks around, as if he misplaced her. "Oh, she came over to crash after her roommate pissed her off. That and she was out of hash. What you up to?"

"I got to talk to you, man," I say. "I think something's wrong with me, but it's hard to talk about."

"Well, take a seat. Just toss her feet off the end of the couch there. She won't notice."

The deep bronze of Laura's calves tell me that's not a good idea. "I'd rather sit on the floor."

"Whatever. So you sick?"

"Not exactly. More like crazy."

"Yeah, I'm nuts, too."

"I'm being serious." I can barely keep from gagging, but the air's a little better close to the floor. "I really think I've lost it. Or. . ."

"Or?" Sade asks.

"Or the Devil's messing with me."

"What devil?"

"You know, *the* Devil."

"You mean the one with a tail and cow feet?" Sade snorts into his yellow-stained glass.

"No, the Prince of Darkness and King of Lies, you jerk." I tell him the whole story. Except for the embarrassing parts.

"You been reading the back of too many damn comic books," he says. He takes a sip from his yellowing glass.

"I don't read comic books."

"You know, all those stupid ads in old comic books. Like for fake vomit and hand buzzers. They always had those X-ray glasses with a picture of a guy looking through some girl's dress." He wipes the drops of fluid from his red goatee.

"But that was crap. This is for real."

"Maybe it's just bad acid. I swear every time I go to the movies now the curtains look like they're moving. I tell everybody 'Hey, look at the curtains move,' and they all look at me like I'm crazy."

I don't say anything. I made my confession; I can't help it if the prick won't believe me. I glance over at Laura in the hopes that she's now fully clothed, but from her pale and arousing stomach I can tell there's no change.

"How about my sister?" Sade asks.

Damn, he saw me look at her. I don't answer, but the searing heat in my face is answer enough.

"Have you ever seen my sister naked before?"

"No!"

"But she's nude right now."

"Yes."

"Prove it."

"How?"

"What's she got tattooed on her inner left thigh?"

"I'm not going to look at your sister's inner thigh." Although.

"Well, then at least look at this, boy scout." Sade tosses his glass to the floor and roughly pushes Laura on to her side so that her back is facing us. He points to her lower back, right where the spine ends and a long crevice begins. "What you see there?"

"A gothic cross laced with black roses."

Sade drops his sister carelessly back on to the couch and lowers himself back into the recliner. "Doesn't prove anything. You could've easily picked that up from the one thousand and one guys who have seen her naked."

"But I didn't; that's what I saw."

"What'd you see?" Laura's sitting up on her elbows. Her eyes move along the red faults spreading from the translucent green of her irises, first to Sade's wicked grin then to my reddening forehead.

"Richie's got X-ray vision; he can see right through your nickers."

Damn you, Sade.

Laura's breasts, big as grapefruit, heave as she draws in the acidic air in a long yawn. "Do you like what you see?" She lets one of her legs drop to the floor and reclines in a melodramatically seductive manner. I turn to Sade for help.

"Don't look at me. She's a big girl." He picks up his fiery glass and adds, "I'm going to bed. Laura, make sure

I'm up by midnight; Francesca's coming over." Sade steps into the hallway, and I hear a door shut.

What a big help. Where do I go now?

"Well?" Laura's legs dangle over the arm of the couch as she reaches for a half-smoked cigarette resting on the lip of a peanut butter jar lid.

"I have to go."

"Before you go, can you be a gentleman and hand me the lighter?"

To get the lighter I'd have to bend over the couch. "I really gotta go. Sorry."

She's yelling to her brother about his "shitty friends" as I cough out into the bright sunshine.

Part IV: Paradise in a Pair of Blue Jeans

I wish I could say I spent the rest of the day in quiet contemplation of my problem, struggling with the demons inside me. Unfortunately, I can't since what I actually did was rent a Cindy Crawford workout video and eat a pepperoni pizza. After all, I can't be expected to defeat the Devil. That's Rev. Johnston's job, and he'll be earning his money here in a moment.

The night meetings are held in a smaller room in the serpentine complex behind the church proper. It takes five minutes to find the right one. It takes another fifteen for anyone else to show up.

The seats are the fold-up kind arranged in semicircles. Mrs. Henderson takes a seat in the row in front of me; I take the Rolaids I pocketed for the occasion. The seats fill rapidly, and soon I hear someone plop beside me.

"Making up for all that lost time?"

It's that plain girl from this morning. She's gone to the trouble to look even plainer by pulling her wild hair into a strict ponytail. "Just interested in the topic."

"What was your name again?" She smells of toothpaste.

"Richard Corry." Leave me alone. I'm trying to have a religious experience here. Why is she looking at me like that? Oh. "What's yours?"

"Mary Stein."

"Pleased to met you." Just as pleased to see the small mole on the side of your right thigh.

"I'm scared to death of the Devil. I saw that movie where the girl's head spun around. You know the one?" She asks.

"*The Exorcist*."

"Yeah, that's it. Anyway, I saw that and that's the scariest movie I've ever seen. I can't believe how frightened I got over a movie. Anyway, I've been afraid of being possessed ever since. That's why I came."

Well, that was a scary movie, but I think my real life problem is a bit more serious than some Hollywood make-believe. But that does give me an idea. "Where would you find an exorcist?"

"Blockbuster's got it."

Oh, boy. "No, the real exorcists."

"I don't remember who played him. I don't think he was real famous."

Scared of the Devil are you? "You know, I'm possessed."

She smiles; her teeth are gappy.

"Really, the Devil's possessed me," I say.

"Your head's not turning in circles." She giggles in an annoyingly high pitch.

"No, it's hard to explain, but the Devil really has done something to me."

"It's all right, Brother. We're all beset by the Devil now and again," a balding man in a blue suit says as he pats my shoulder and moves toward the next row.

I'm talking too loud.

"Have you seen that movie?" she asks.

"Yeah, but what's that got to do with it?"

"So you got scared, too?" She looks scared.

"No... yes, but.... Look the Devil's cursed me. I think he's trying to drive me insane, so he can get my soul."

"How can he get your soul by making you crazy?" She bites her lower lip when she concentrates, but her eyes never move from mine.

"I always thought that when my time was coming I'd just get saved on the spur of the moment. Of course, if I'm nuts, I won't know what to do, so I'll end up in hell." I'm worried about her lip. She's biting it hard enough to draw blood.

"How's he driving you crazy?"

"Let's just say it has to do with the Devil's bad fashion sense." She's smiling again. She probably thinks it's all a joke. At least she stopped biting her lip.

Rev. Johnston comes in and launches into an attack on the Devil cloaked in all walks of life: movies, TV, music, science, politics, doctors, lawyers, homosexuals, and all the rest of the usuals but nothing about naked women in general or people who suddenly can only see naked women in specific. I begin to despair until he goes into the closing prayer. It runs half as long as the sermon and reads like a banishment from a Puritan of Old who knew Hell was in the next forest over.

I close my eyes and say a fervent "Amen" but see only the freckles on Mary's leg when I open my eyes. So much for my last best hope at "First Hope." It's just not fair. And not only for me. Here Mary is being nice to me. Hell, she's the only person who's tried to understand or even to listen. I shouldn't be looking at her like this, not without her knowing it. She deserves respect, but all I can think of is her small breasts.

"So is the Devil gone?"

"No." Maybe I can learn to live with an increased libido. I can join the circus and set up a "Guess Your Pubic Hair Color" booth. Bound to be plenty of ways I can capitalize on this sort of thing.

"Are you afraid?" Mary asks in a whisper, leaning into me.

"I don't know."

Mary reaches over slowly and takes my hand. I don't know what to do. I usually avoid touching other people. Her palm's sweaty. The air gets caught in my throat. She just as slowly rests the back of my hand on her leg a little above the knee. Breathe dammit. There's only so much a guy can take. I close my eyes bracing for the smooth touch of her leg, though it looks about as smooth as sand paper.

But instead I feel the coarse texture of blue jeans, not skin, or even stubble. White splotches explode in kaleidoscope-fashion around my eyes, but I refuse to open them. What if it's only my vision that's broken? Maybe the Devil's screwing with me again. What if I can feel this woman's clothes, but when I open my eyes she's still naked? I can't take that. I could blind myself and go around feeling clothed women.

Through the white spots swirling in the black of my eyelids, I can see patterns forming. Huge concentric circles spinning around and around. Each circle another color. Colors I'd never seen, but felt like I could remember. The spinning circles pulsate and enlarge, the outer ones disappearing and the dot in the center releasing more and more circles. I'm falling, falling into the circles. I fall into the circles, but they slow and stop. The circles turn into arms and hands held tightly together. A man and a woman holding hands and twirling, skipping around, but not letting the circle break. Damn creepy.

Slowly, through squinting eyes, I look at Mary's chest and see a white t-shirt. The slight swell of her breasts is much more alluring under a shirt. And the way her jeans cling to her thighs. Wait–if she's dressed, I must be cured. I leap out of my seat to see all around me clothed women. Bright blouses, dark skirts, light shirts, creased slacks, flowery dresses, cream suits, black hose, white tennis shoes, brown high heels. I am in heaven.

Mrs. Henderson is now garbed in a dress almost as hideous as her thighs, but I'd kiss her on the mouth if I could reach her. I reach for Mary instead. I grab her hand and pull her up and out of the church, past the throng of beautifully attired women slowly moving for the exit or Rev. Johnston.

"Have you gone crazy?" Mary asks.

We walk to the playground near the church with slides, swings, and a push merry-go-round. The scattered oaks nod in the wind to us as to old friends. We sit next to each other on the old merry-go-round, and it squeaks as we gently turn it with our feet.

As I get caught in the wilderness of Mary's hair, I whisper, "My Beatrice."

She pushes me off her. "What'd you call me?"